CITY *of* the DEAD
and
BAYOU DOGS

TONY ABBOTT

SCHOLASTIC INC.

NEW YORK TORONTO LONDON AUCKLAND SYDNEY
MEXICO CITY NEW DELHI HONG KONG BUENOS AIRES

The Haunting of Derek Stone #1: City of the Dead
ISBN 0-545-03429-9, copyright © 2009 by Robert T. Abbott.
The Haunting of Derek Stone #2: Bayou Dogs
ISBN 0-545-03430-2, copyright © 2009 by Robert T. Abbott.

These books were originally published by Apple Paperbacks.

ISBN-13: 978-0-545-15368-3
ISBN-10: 0-545-15368-9

12 11 10 9 8 7 6 5 4 3 2 1 9 10 11 12 13 14/0

Printed in the U.S.A. 40

First compilation printing, January 2009

3.7

CITY *of the* DEAD

To Those No Longer Here

CONTENTS

ONE

What Happened on the Train

I'll tell you straight: The dead are coming back.

You won't believe it, of course. You'll say it's crazy. It's impossible. It's whatever.

Fine. I get it. Most of the time I don't believe it myself. But it's happening, and it affects all of us.

If you're smart, you'll listen and be afraid.

If you're really smart, you'll run.

And you'll do it now, because pretty soon there won't be anywhere to run to.

I'm going to tell you everything that happened from the moment my father, my brother, and I stepped onto the train. That's probably a good place to begin. I say "probably" because I'm not sure exactly when this story did begin. Maybe it was ten years ago. Maybe it was ten thousand years ago.

But never mind that now. You need some facts.

My name is Derek Stone. I'm fourteen and just finished eighth grade. I live in New Orleans, Louisiana. I'm a little chunky. I have pimples on my chin, but not too bad. The hearing in my left ear is not good because of an infection I had when I was young. My hands are small for my age. I don't have many friends. My GPA is 4.27.

So what? So nothing. I'm telling you everything.

For years it's been just my father; my brother, Ronny; and me. Ronny is five years older than I am. We've been pretty close since he finished high school because he still lives at home. My mother left ten years ago. She said Dad was away too much, so she moved to Paris to be even farther away. Yeah, I don't get it, either.

There's one more thing you'll need to know: I don't make things up. I don't *imagine*. I don't day-dream. I like real stuff. True things. Up is up. Down is down. Fire is hot. Water is wet. I like what I can trust.

That's it, then. You know enough for me to start.

It was late afternoon on a Saturday when my dad, my brother, and I raced onto the train in Alexandria, Louisiana. Alexandria is a couple hundred miles northwest of New Orleans. We wouldn't normally be on a train, but we took one then because the day was all about trains.

My father is . . . was . . . a nut about vintage rail-road stock, the kind that rumbled through our state until about thirty years ago. North to south, east to west, they puffed black coal and white steam into the humid air. Dad loved old-fashioned locomotives. He had collected little models of them for as long as I could remember. He had tried forever to convince me and Ronny to go with him to the annual TrainMania convention. We never wanted to go, but we went this year because he really begged us and because it meant so much to him and because we were both too lazy to concoct another excuse. So fine. We went.

Imagine:

It was just after six in the evening and hot in the Third Street station, the way only a late June day could be. We flew through the gate, nearly missing the train because Dad had dawdled at the convention. He couldn't decide which of three model trains to buy, but he finally ended up with a replica of a 1928 Southern Arrow. The three of us had just jumped through the train door into the end car when the train gave a great screech. The last call for the 6:10 to New Orleans sounded over the address system.

Whistling like a kid, Dad dived into one of the two open benches and slapped the seat next to him. "Derek, here, left side. Ronny, on the aisle."

I slid between Dad and the window, with my good

ear to him. He was pumped, but I was exhausted from a full day of squeezing through aisle after aisle in a giant hall full of train geeks. For one thing, I hated the nonstop noise. For another, I was sweaty and tired. I'm not all that light on my feet, and running through the train station wasn't my idea of a good time.

Ronny sat on the aisle. Two soldiers in full fatigues took the bench seat opposite us.

Does all this matter? You decide.

Ronny and I had this gag going, which started during our race to the station. I pretended to be a cranky old man trying to get the last seat, and Ronny kept calling for "Mr. Conductor" in a British accent. We fooled around with this again until the train squealed a second time, ready to set off, and the doors started to close.

All of a sudden, a mother and daughter stumbled through the doors and stood panting in the aisle, breathless from running and clutching handfuls of shopping bags. The girl was about my age. Along with everything else, she was holding a pastry box tied with white and red string. I remember it because of what happened later.

The doors hissed shut. The train groaned a third time and began to roll. When it did, the two soldiers turned to see the girl and her mother. One of them —

a short, wiry guy with a thin face — sprang from his seat, nudging his buddy to get up, too.

"Take our seats," he said, bowing and waving his hand at the open seats.

"Please," said the other one. He was tall and had shoulders as wide as a baseball bat. As giant as he was, he had a full, round, laughing face. He looked as if he were in the middle of telling a story that he couldn't get to the end of without cracking up. "Please sit."

"Thank you," said the mother. She and her daughter sat down opposite us, while the two soldiers stood in the open area near the doors.

The moment we pulled out of the station, a block of orange light slanted between the buildings and across the girl's face. She blinked and turned her head away. I don't know if that means anything. I'm only saying that the sun was starting to set. That was some of the last of it we saw that day.

Dad unwrapped the Southern Arrow train model and studied it.

Oh, right. Here's something else. Dad loved trains, but he sold boats. He sold boats, but he didn't like the water. I guess I inherited that from him. No. That's not right. Genetics has nothing to do with it. I had a thing about water because once — no, never mind.

I'll tell you that later.

Ronny, though, was a fish. All through high school he was the best swimmer. The swim team won the state championship twice while he was captain. He must have gotten his love of water from Mom. Mom loved to swim. She swam right out of our lives ten years ago. But I already said that.

The girl's name was Abby, the girl across from us. I remember because her mother said, "Abby, can you reach up and put my bags on the upper . . . thing?"

I remember thinking she probably wanted to say "luggage rack," but couldn't think of the words.

So the girl's name was Abby. Remember that.

Dad rose from his seat to help her put the bags up.

Me, I wasn't doing anything special. I had a book in my lap, but wasn't reading it. After we settled in, Dad turned back to his miniature train and started talking about all the old stock that once crisscrossed the South. He knew a lot about them, from the Civil War on. The Del Monte, the Owl, the Golden Rocket, the Coaster, the Klamath, the Argonaut. I didn't mind listening to Dad go on. It was his day, after all. I glanced past him at Ronny, who actually asked decent questions. Dad swallowed them up, telling us everything he knew as if we'd never asked before — which we hadn't.

About an hour into the ride, when things had quieted down and I had begun my book, Abby laughed at something.

I glanced up.

Her mother was pretending to open the cheesecake box on the sly, while Abby pretended to keep catching her.

Maybe it was the fun of the day, or maybe because the mother was acting silly, but Dad abruptly came out with: "Excuse me, ladies, it seems like you need some help with that cheesecake. Maybe I'd better hold it for you . . ."

They both looked up, astonished that we had caught them playing their little game.

"Dad!" I groaned, embarrassed.

But Abby and her mother burst into laughter. "No! No!" they chimed.

Ronny and I laughed, too.

As near as I remember, that was when Dad arched up in his seat. His eyes were fixed on something outside the window beside me.

"What is it?" I asked, following his gaze.

"This bridge we're going to cross," he said. "It goes back to the nineteen-thirties. The Southern Arrow probably crossed it a thousand times. I have some great books about old bridges, if you guys are interested. Wow, is this beautiful!"

We all looked. The bridge was a neat assembly of steel girders hatch-marked against the dark blue sky. The trestles below the tracks were pale silver, streaked with lines of rust from the bolts dotting the seams. It looked old.

We felt a bump as our car rolled across the tracks onto the bridge. The rumbling over the steel rails was loud and hollow. As the train moved over the span, the girders flashed slowly by the window to my left — light, shadow, light, shadow. The bridge curved slightly to the left, so leaning against the window I could see the engine roll onto the far side. Then the first car was on land. The second. It was strange watching the train move like a snake across the air.

As our car rolled toward the middle of the span, I saw the reason for the bridge through the trestles beneath us: a deep chasm between two steep, rocky slopes, with a dark river at the bottom. I turned away when my legs tingled uncomfortably.

"Do you have a place for the Southern Arrow in your collection?" asked Ronny, nodding at the model in Dad's lap. "In your special room?"

"All picked out," Dad said. "I'm going to —"

A sudden shudder went through the car, a feeling as if the whole weight of the train had shifted backward heavily. Then a sound like wrenching iron. I looked at Dad. His mouth was open, his eyes dark.

"Dad —" I said.

"The bridge —" he started. "Oh . . . no . . ."

The car sank, still rolling forward. Some people shouted. The conductor stumbled between the seats to the door that connected our car to the one in front of us. But our car dropped backward again. He was thrown to the floor, and we were all pushed back into our seats.

The conductor hung on to the seat backs and made a sound in his throat. "We're falling!"

TWO

The Fall

The train car tilted suddenly to the left, setting off an alarm on the public address system.

Abby screamed. The cake slid off her lap toward Ronny's feet. Out of reflex, he lurched to catch it, missed, and fell forward almost into her. As the cake splattered onto the floor, something slammed — hard — into the roof of the car. I saw a girder twist away from the bridge and fly past the window on my left. People screamed.

I gripped my seat. Ronny struggled to stand up, then slid halfway down the aisle toward the back of the car.

"Ronny!" I shouted. It sounded like a little boy yelling, not my voice at all. "Ronny!"

"Hold on to something! Everybody!" one of the soldiers yelled, clinging to the luggage rack to hold himself up.

"Derek, grab the seat," yelled Dad, who had fallen

to the floor in the aisle. He was on his back, face red, struggling like a beetle to right himself.

Everything was tumbling toward the rear of the car.

I grabbed the underside of my seat and held tight. Abby's purse struck my face and scratched my cheek. Her mother tumbled into my seat, then flew right over my head toward the rear of the car. There was a sickening groan, then nothing.

"Mom!" Abby yelled.

Something snapped loudly, and the car fell like a dead weight. My stomach lurched to my throat. Screams echoed all around me. We saw the trestles receding above us.

We were in free-fall.

An instant later, the back end of the train struck the side of the ravine, crunching into the side of the rocks. It stuck there for a moment before flipping toward the chasm. The windows on both sides of the car exploded, spraying glass into the cabin. Suddenly, up was down and everyone slammed up to the ceiling and back again. My shoulder felt crushed. I smelled vomit.

A shaft of iron broke off from somewhere and shot through the cabin like a spear. I tried to duck out of the way, but now Dad was sprawled across my legs. I didn't know where Ronny had gone. I jammed my head down and squeezed my eyes shut. Then I felt it.

The iron shaft struck me behind the left ear like an icicle.

I blanked for a second. Warm fluid poured across my cheek, into my eyes. Ronny's hand was suddenly on my back, holding me down between the seats. He shouted in my ear, but I didn't hear what he said.

The train car stuttered down the ravine. Sparks the size of baseballs shot out the front of the cabin. I caught a glimpse of the girl, Abby, nearly upside down. She was pinned between the last row of seats and the rear door.

I couldn't believe I wasn't dead. I was still seeing things happen around me. Things I could never imagine people doing.

"Dad —" I called. "Ronny!"

The cabin suddenly surged up. The car folded onto itself, twisted backward, then buckled. One half of it ripped off and dangled on the hillside. I saw Dad slide away, down the aisle and out of sight, screaming at the top of his lungs. Our half of the car tumbled once, then stopped.

The stop was so sudden that the moment it happened — and I remember this part clearly — Ronny flew at the window next to me as if he was aiming for it. It was the strangest movement I'd ever seen.

"Derek! Derek! Help! Help —"

His mouth was wide open, but fell silent as he flew into the black chasm below.

Flame and dust clouded around me, around everything. The air was a deafening roar. It went black inside my head.

THREE

At Bordelon Gap

I was nowhere for a long time. At least, I'm told it was a long time. I don't really know.

When I finally opened my eyes, I was sprawled on the ground. It was dark except for a bright orange light flaring somewhere below me. People were screaming, crying, yelling all around. My nose stung with the smell of burning rubber.

"This one's moving," someone called out. "Frankie, he's breathing. Bring a stretcher! Medic, over here —"

Feeling came back into my limbs, and I realized I was lying on steeply sloped ground, my head toward the top of the slope. There were people and search-lights and shouting and a roaring from below. I wanted to prop myself up on my elbows, look into the chasm. When I tried, someone held me down.

"Hold on a second," said a woman. "Don't move. We have to check you over. Can you feel your legs?"

"My head hurts, my neck," I said. The pain where

the iron shaft struck me felt like a burning dagger behind my left ear. "I can't see too well."

"It's blood in your eyes," someone said.

If I'd understood, I would have been grossed out by that. But I didn't understand. Couldn't.

For the next few minutes they examined me. After they cleaned my face and eyes, my vision focused. Pain seared through my ear and into my head.

"Bruises on his face, shoulder, both knees, neck behind his left ear, possible concussion," a man said, patting a piece of gauze in a spot above my eyebrows that didn't hurt much at all. He wore rubber gloves. I smelled the latex. He pressed his fingers along my arms and legs, my stomach.

"Any of this hurt, really hurt?" he asked me.

It didn't. I shook my head.

"What's your name?" the woman asked.

"Derek," I said. "Derek Stone." My voice didn't sound like me.

"Were you traveling with anybody?"

"My father and my brother. Where's Ronny?" I croaked, trying to get up again.

"Hold on," she said, holding me down.

"Ronny! Dad!" I tried to yell, but only a hoarse whisper came out. My voice was gone. I remembered screaming all through the crash. It was catching up to me.

A loud hissing noise cut through the air as water was pumped from hoses at the fire below. At the burning railcar.

A rectangular shape swung slowly over my head, outlined by bright light.

It looked like a coffin with a halo. It was a stretcher.

"Girl, unconscious," said a technician a few feet away. "They're taking her to one of the rescue vans."

I shut my eyes to dampen the pain, then blinked them open. "The brown-haired girl?" I said, not remembering her name.

"She kept talking about 'him.' I don't know 'him,' but I guess someone helped her," he said. "She was on the edge of the ravine."

"Her mother? Is her mother okay?" I asked.

"There's someone on the rocks below," the man went on, staring into the black depths. "Somebody said they saw her, a woman."

I gazed down, squinting through the darkness. The thin strip of a river ran along the bottom of the chasm. It was black and alive, glinting silver from the lights. "Dark river," I said.

"What?" the woman asked, leaning to me.

I looked at her. "I don't know. 'Dark river, of many deaths.' That's a line, right?"

"A line of what?" she asked.

I blinked. "I don't know."

"More lights are coming soon," said a fireman, holding my arm to keep me from falling. I hadn't noticed him until then. "As far as we can tell, there are nine missing. We're doing all we can to get to them —"

"Good luck! That's the Red River down there," someone else chimed in. He had no uniform, but wore thick ropes over both shoulders and danced nervously from foot to foot. "Bordelon Gap is a hundred feet straight to the water and no more than five feet wide at the bottom. It's a sheer drop a long way . . ." He shuttled off impatiently without finishing.

"A Marine climbing crew is on its way," one of the EMS workers said to someone, not me. "They'll rappel down the ravine. The governor's called them in. We need to get these others to the hospital. Frankie, here —"

I wasn't getting it.

"Where are Ronny and Dad?" I asked, out loud this time. No one said anything.

"Put me in the same van as my brother and father," I demanded, feeling a tug at the back of my mind and hoping I would be awake to hear the response. Things got blurry.

Sirens wailed. Worse, I heard people moaning

from somewhere down the slope. Why weren't they being helped? The air stank of burned rubber, scorched oil, and a sulphurlike smell that made my eyes tear. A small army of men in jumpsuits was climbing slowly down to the edge of the ravine.

Out of the corner of my eye, I saw the water down below again, glinting in the searchlights. It was moving among the sharp rocks, always moving.

River of many deaths . . .

"It's all rocks," one of the men near me said. "We've gone over everything. I'm sorry."

"Sorry? You weren't driving the train," I said. But that wasn't what they were sorry about. It was Ronny and Dad. They weren't on the slope with me. They weren't above the ravine. They were down there. In the chasm. On the rocks. In the river. Gone.

"I'm sorry," the man said again.

The world shifted. All I wanted was for our train to be back in New Orleans.

"Come with us, up the hill," someone said gently. "Let's get you on a stretcher."

"No, no. No!"

"Come with us," someone said, sliding me onto a gurney. Two men lifted it up.

"No —" My throat filled with cotton, my head went light. I leaned over the gurney and got sick on the ground.

I had survived a horrific accident with barely a bump on my head, but my brother and my father hadn't?

They were gone?

They were dead?

FOUR

Grief

They tell me a hospital upstate played pincushion with me for two full days. I was hooked up to a half-dozen monitors. I went through CAT scans, head-to-toe physicals, blood tests, X-rays, cardiograms. My blood pressure was monitored constantly.

I don't remember any of it.

They also tell me I called for Dad and Ronny about a million times, but I don't remember that, either.

While I was out, I kept seeing one particular moment of the crash. So many things were unclear, but I could see this perfectly.

It was when the car twisted and Ronny was thrown at the glassless window next to me. In that instant, his face filled with horror and surprise. His eyes locked with mine.

"Derek! Derek! Help! Help —"

But there was something I couldn't wrap my head around. It was the way his arms went up and out the window. They went straight out the window and then he jerked up, as if he were being pulled out of the cabin.

Pulled?

Impossible.

I began to surface on the third day of tests. The doctors were frowning, then surprised. Then they gave me more tests.

At some point, I heard that the girl — I remembered now that her name was Abby — was in a coma on another floor. She had possible brain damage and was not expected to survive.

They called her the Donner girl.

Abby Donner.

The press, I discovered, was all over the crash, hounding the survivors, haunting the hospitals. When no one could find anything more to treat, they let my dad's brother check me out. I don't know how, but Uncle Carl got me through the parking garage and into his car without running into a single reporter, photographer, or cameraman.

Carl Stone was an okay guy. He and my dad hadn't seen each other much over the last few years since Carl had moved to Oregon, where he owned a software business. But he was back, he said, for as long as I needed. That was comforting.

Around the time I left the hospital, the newspapers

discovered that this was "the second crash at the same site," and an investigation was launched into the building of the bridge. It had been built in 1936, a government project, so the investigation went nowhere except into history. Who cared about that, anyway? It made no difference now. My whole family was gone in a single evening.

Carl drove me home to New Orleans. It was a silent trip.

It was only when I saw the skyline and smelled the river that it really hit me. My brother and my father weren't going to be home as usual.

According to the media, they were "missing and presumed dead," part of a group of nine victims who were "missing and presumed dead." But you know what that means.

They were just dead.

Dad had told me it always amazed him how quickly I had understood and accepted that Mom had left us.

"France?" I had said. "That's where the Eiffel Tower is. And funny cars. Nice for Mommy." I was four.

Dad had said that on that day I had closed the hole that her departure had opened in my life. I never asked when she would be back. I understood fully that she wouldn't.

So.

Now my brother and my father were gone, too.

And I was alone.

"Here we are, Derek," Carl said, as we slowed on Royal Street. It was midday, the very end of June, and the street was as lively as ever.

"It'll get better," Carl added softly. "Day by day."

"Sure," I said.

I climbed out of the car and stood in front of my house while he parked around the corner.

My house. Right. You should know about it.

Royal Street was an ancient street and 517 was one of its oldest standing addresses, a three-hundred-year-old brick house in the heart of the French Quarter. Royal is packed with noisy jazz clubs and cafés and shops that get even noisier during tourist months. My favorite part of the house was the courtyard on the back alley. It was a jungle of plants, vines, and potted palms. It had a brick patio, two fountains, and a wrought-iron table with chairs in the center. For me, it was always one of the few places in the Quarter where you could actually relax and breathe. Noise from the street faded away when you were walled in back there among the plants.

The second story of the house was balconied over the street with a wrought-iron railing, like the grille of an antique car. At the very top stood what was called a *faux chambre,* a false room. It was shaped like a lantern, with broad windows on each of its eight sides that glared down on the streets. It sat on the roof like a pillbox, its only purpose to balance out the design of the house.

On the very tip of the roof stood a wooden figure of an angel painted gold. Wasn't there some line that went, *Angel child, child of light*? What was that from? My mind was a jumble. I turned to see the other houses on our street with false rooms. Peacocks, deer, frogs, and eagles ornamented their roofs. Dad had told me that while the room was meant just for show, he had made it into a space for his train collection and railroad books. I'd never been up there.

Carl hustled to unlock the front door, and I entered the house. Even when he dropped the keys on the table, made noise in the kitchen, and began to fix lunch, the rooms seemed strangely silent, eerie. I stood in the hallway for ten minutes without moving. I didn't know what to do. Then I went upstairs to Ronny's room.

His swimming trophies neatly lined a glass case on the wall. The rest of the room was as messy as any nineteen-year-old's room. And why not? He thought he was coming back to it.

I went to my room, collapsed on the unmade bed, and fell asleep without eating lunch.

* * *

Over the next few days, I spent a lot of time in the courtyard, doing nothing. There was nothing to say to anyone, anyway. A bridge failed, a train fell, nine people were presumed dead, and rescue workers were still searching for them. That's all. My injuries were minor, considering. The concussion from being hit in the head was the worst because of the headaches, but even those weren't so bad anymore.

A week passed and the search for survivors — and then bodies — ended. Bordelon Gap was too deep and inaccessible, the river too swift. The newspaper and TV reporters went away. There was a tornado in Kansas, an earthquake in China. The world was done with train wrecks. Everyone left us alone.

Carl decided we needed a memorial service of some kind, and that we'd do it at the family tomb. I still found it all hard to swallow. Every day, I expected Dad to call me down for dinner. Any minute, I thought Ronny would barge into my room and tell me something dumb. But I didn't like wishing for something unreal. I didn't like inventing.

Up was up. Down was down.

So on the Saturday two weeks after the crash, we went with a priest to St. Louis Cemetery Number One to say good-bye.

An aboveground warren of small stone houses, alabaster and marble and limestone, St. Louis Cemetery was divided into cramped neighborhoods, narrow streets, and blind alleys like a little city.

In fact, people called it the City of the Dead.

The day was burning hot. The air hung heavy and wet and smelling like damp stone.

Ronny's on-again, off-again girlfriend, Samantha, came with her parents. Short and blond, she had remained friends with Ronny even after their latest breakup.

After crying for a while in the hot, white sun, Sam came up to me. "Did he . . . was it painful, do you think?"

I said I didn't know. Then I remembered what one of the rescuers said. "But he was a hero," I told her. "He saved a girl. Everybody said so. She's alive because of him." I had almost convinced myself that Ronny was the "him" Abby Donner had spoken about before she went into her coma. It was probably a lie, but it hardly mattered.

Sam hung on every word. She nodded, sobbed, blew her nose, sobbed again, and left with her parents before the service was over.

Standing beside the squat white tomb, the priest began to read lots of nice-sounding words from a book, then spoke about a boy and his father. But I could barely breathe and heard almost none of what he went on about, until he mentioned "the dear brothers . . . Derek and Ronny."

Derek and Ronny.

"I miss him," I blubbered to my friend Tooley Calder, who stood next to me.

"I remember all the stuff he did to you," said Tooley quietly.

"Yeah," I said. "But I've wanted to be him forever. My whole life."

A group of mourners was assembling two streets over. I saw a trumpet flash in the sun. I expected to hear a note, but instead, there was a low mumbling sound that went up the side of my neck and behind my left ear. It felt like a needle was being pushed into my damaged eardrum.

"Don't you think?" Tooley asked.

I turned. "Sorry. What?" I said, pressing my ear closed with my finger.

"Don't you think you guys were just so different? Ronny got the brawn. You got all the rest."

I think I smiled. "But he saved that girl on the train."

"The coma girl?" Tooley asked.

I nodded.

I had come to believe my own invention, that Ronny saved Abby Donner, even though "saved" is a big word for someone in a coma. But Tooley was right, mostly. Ronny only ever turned on a computer to play a game, and he didn't know or care where the library was. He had four things in his life: swimming, girls, girls, and swimming. He was popular, thin, good-looking, social, always joking. The opposite of me.

Tooley gave me a little smile. "Makes you wonder how you guys came from the same gene pool, you know?"

I knew. But there were times when Ronny looked sideways at me with that face, the half smile lighting up his eyes as if we shared a private thing. There was something working between us.

He knew me, and I knew him.

And now there was Derek, but there was no Ronny.

Just then, someone started up some kind of grinding engine nearby. Its sound shivered through my legs and feet.

Who would do that?

Who would make that kind of noise in the middle of a funeral service?

The priest kept going as though he hadn't heard,

as though he always went on with the service no matter what. I turned in every direction, but saw no engine. It rumbled the ground under my feet and rose up into my chest.

"What is that noise?" I asked Tooley.

"Shh," he said, nodding at the priest, who was looking at me and smiling.

I returned his smile. I guess he had said my name, since others were looking at me, too.

It meant nothing.

Then the trumpet shot out a note and really did interrupt the service. Heads turned. It sounded like a dagger splitting through the air. The priest paused, then went on.

My face was draining into my chest, my stomach, my knees. Carl held me up on one side, Tooley on the other.

An hour after I kissed the tomb that contained neither Dad nor Ronny, I was finally home, feeling as dead as they were.

The next few days rolled by in a blur. I hope nothing important happened, because I don't remember much of it. What I do remember is that I met, shook hands with, was hugged by, had my cheeks pinched by, and forgot the names of dozens and dozens of family friends.

What did I care about them?

When the last person left our house, I felt like bolting the door and never leaving again. I wanted to close my eyes and see nothing.

Forget it all.

Sleep for a hundred years.

But sleep wasn't any good, either.

FIVE

The Coming

I started to tell you before about me and water, about what happened to make me hate water more than just about anything. Sometimes I think that maybe it never really happened. That it's my own little nightmare, a horrifying memory cooked up for some reason I can't remember.

But it might as well have happened, since I'm completely terrified of dark swamps, churning rivers, and all the black watery depths that you find scattered everywhere around our ancient state.

And the dogs, of course. There are always the dogs.

The nightmare came back my first night home after the accident. And again every night after that.

Every night, the same nightmare.

And every morning, the same sickness in my stomach.

Uncle Carl did his best, but how could anyone deal with this? Even while I was in the hospital, Carl had attempted to get in touch with my mother. He'd had the U.S. Embassy try to contact her in France. There were e-mails, phone calls, cables, letters, even messengers, but she was away. No one knew exactly where. So two and a half weeks after the accident, she still didn't know. If she'd known, she would have come back — wouldn't she?

In the meantime, Carl stayed in the house with me. One day, he came out to the courtyard. As usual, I was sitting silent and alone and looking at nothing.

"Can you do your brother's room?"

That's what he said. *Do your brother's room.* I didn't understand. "Sorry?"

"Go through Ronny's room, clean it up a little?" Carl said, looking not at me, but at the bricks on the patio floor. He was holding a stack of Dad's shirts. Then his eyes met mine. "You know, it's been almost three weeks. It should be straightened up. If you think you can. Maybe pack some of his things in boxes?"

In boxes? Oh, man.

I understood. Of course, I did. But I couldn't. Messing with Ronny's stuff, the swimming trophies, the junk in his desk, his dresser, packing up his clothes, his socks? It would mean I didn't expect him to come right back.

"Can't it wait?" I said.

Carl smiled gently. "Sure. No problem. No big deal."

The way he said it made me feel ungrateful for all the time he was spending here, away from his home.

"No," I said. "It's all right. I'll do it."

He breathed in. "If you can. It might help to work through, you know, him not being here? Anyway, just a little. To start."

I did start little. I started slow. Every single thing of Ronny's, no matter how trivial, flooded me with memories of stuff we used to do together. It took me an hour to move a sock, a magazine, a CD.

Then, just before I was about to give up for the day, I heard a long, drawn-out note. A low sound, almost like the rumbling I had heard in the cemetery. In the quiet of Ronny's room, though, I heard it more clearly. It didn't sound like a machine this time.

It sounded like . . . voices. Lots of them. A chorus of voices, confused, overlapping, wild, low.

They were moaning.

I shivered, dropped my hands from the dresser knobs, and listened. I thought about the moaning at the ravine. It was louder in my left ear, the bad one, just as I'd heard it in the cemetery. I put my finger in my ear, stopped it up, then released it. The sound moved away. Turned a corner. Then it was back again, nearer. I whirled around to face the hallway. There was no one there.

Of course there was no one there.

I stepped into the hall. The sound was nearer still, but was so deep. It seemed impossible for voices to be that low. It was like something primal. Uh-huh. Right. Maybe that concussion had been worse than I'd thought.

"Who's there?" I said, intending my words to be louder.

No answer.

"Uncle Carl?" I said. That was a whisper, too. Like when I called out in my nightmare. Calling, desperate to be heard, but afraid to wake anyone. "Carl?"

No answer. I went to the landing at the top of the stairs.

"Uncle Carl?" I called down. "Are you listening to music?"

"Huh?"

I turned quickly. He was in the hall behind me. His arms were draped with my dad's neckties.

The voices softened, drew back.

"Are you listening to music?" I asked again.

He glanced behind him. "No. What do you hear?"

"Nothing," I said quickly. "Never mind."

"You all right?" Carl asked. "You know, you don't

have to do Ronny's room if you don't want to. It can wait. You look a little pale."

I was shaking all over. "I'm okay," I said.

But I wasn't okay. I was hearing things. My skull ached. Maybe I really did some kind of serious damage to my head in the accident. Maybe I'm really hurt. Maybe —

"No, I'm fine," I said, going back to Ronny's bedroom.

A little later, the phone rang. Carl was in the bathroom, and I didn't feel like answering it.

"Let it go," he called out from behind the door.

I let it go. You don't answer phones when your brother and your father die on the same day.

A second call. I sat on Ronny's bed, two feet from the phone, listening to the rings until they ended. Not long after, I heard a police siren whooping into the Quarter. I went to Ronny's window and looked down at the curb. The police car had stopped in front of my house. The whirling lights flicked off.

When the car door opened, a man climbed out of the backseat. He stepped awkwardly onto the sidewalk and stood at the curb. Then he slowly lifted his head and looked up.

My chest nearly exploded when I saw his face.

It was Ronny.

SIX

The Impossible Begins

Blood drained from my head. My knees nearly gave out.

I screamed down the stairs, tripping over my own feet, and fell flat on my face in the hall as the door cracked open.

"Ronny!"

His head poked in.

"Ronny!" I cried. He stepped in, squinting at me on the floor. I jumped up and hugged him. "Ronny! Ronny!"

I hugged my lost brother, my brother who everyone thought was dead, my brother who had gone through who-knows-what for nearly a month, and who had come back home, my brother.

But when I wrapped my arms around him, Ronny was ice cold, stiff, awkward. He felt like a tree. Wooden. Except that wood feels more alive than he did just then.

I pulled away. He looked down at me, frowning

strangely. Okay, he was in shock. Of course, he was. Think of what he'd been through!

Two police officers stood behind Ronny. One was grim-faced, somber, the other looked tired. They were both searching my face for something. I couldn't tell what.

"Come in! Oh my gosh, come in!" called Carl, practically throwing himself down the stairs. He half-laughed, half-cried. "Ronny —" His cheeks were wet with tears.

The officers stayed on the doorstep for a few minutes. They told us that Ronny had been found wandering near the ravine, had violently refused medical treatment, and had wanted only to come home. He had apparently gotten into a house somewhere and had been hiding and sleeping in the basement there for days, surviving on who-knows-what. Once the owner found out who he was, he didn't press charges.

Ronny peered past me into the house, almost like we weren't talking about him. One of the officers said that a social worker would call. Then the two men looked from one to the other as if there were more to say, but they didn't say it. Instead, they turned to leave.

"Thank you!" Carl gushed again and again as the officers climbed into their car.

We pulled Ronny inside and closed the door. He stepped back from Carl, gazing at him with a strange, distant look. He's traumatized, I told myself. Falling so far out of a crashing train. Maybe he hit his head. Maybe, in his shock, he didn't remember much. But he was home.

"You were dead," I told him, not finding the right words. "Everyone thinks you're dead, I mean. We have to tell people! How did you get out of there? How did you live through that? Where have you been?" I couldn't stop talking.

"I don't know," Ronny said, shifting nervously from foot to foot. "Just lucky, I guess. Lucky to be here." He chuckled, or tried to. It sounded like a cough. His eyes darted around, never fixing on any one thing.

This was some kind of trauma, right? Couldn't the police have insisted on medical treatment?

We took Ronny's arms and led him into the house.

"No, really," said Carl, pulling him into the kitchen. "Ronny, how did you get out of there?"

He shrugged. "I really don't know."

"Did you see Dad?" I blurted out.

He gave me a weird look. "How'd you know about him?"

"What?" I said. "What do you mean?"

"How do you know about Daddy Jubal?"

"Daddy Jubal?" I said, glancing at Carl. "Who is —"

"Right, right," Ronny said quickly. He almost looked embarrassed. "Dad. Our father. My father. Dad," he said insistently. "So he isn't here?"

Carl and I shared a look.

"The police said your father probably died in the accident," Carl said, pulling out a chair. "We don't know for sure. They haven't found any trace of him."

A worried look came over Ronny's face, starting at his forehead and sliding down to his chin.

"But they might still find him," I said. "If you made it, maybe Dad did, too."

"Oh," Ronny said. "Uh-huh, uh-huh." He didn't sit, but turned and walked out of the kitchen.

"Where is he going?" Carl whispered.

I followed Ronny. I touched his arm, but he pulled it away and climbed upstairs, leaving me at the bottom.

"He's been in an accident," said Carl.

"I know . . ." I said.

"I actually thought you'd be more like this when you came home," Carl said. "Let's give Ronny some space. And time."

Still, I followed Ronny up the stairs into his room. "Sorry for moving your stuff," I said. "I know how you like your things in certain places. We — Uncle Carl and I — didn't hear anything for a long time . . . you know . . ."

"Whatever," Ronny said coldly. He tossed a trophy onto the floor and flopped down on his bed. His eyes were blank, searching the ceiling. "Tell Momma I have to sleep. You can go now."

"Momma?"

"Whoever!" he snapped. "Don't you have mice to trap? Get out."

I stepped backward out of the room, and closed the door. Mice to trap? Something was wrong with Ronny. He was . . . changed. I don't know. I'm not telling this right.

All I knew was that something was wrong with Ronny, and it scared the life out of me.

SEVEN

The Wrong Things

At first, Ronny was all over the news.

The press had a field day with the boy who had survived the "death crash" and the "death chasm" and every other "death" thing.

But Ronny had nothing to say. Nothing. Reporters shoved microphones in his face; he shied away from them, staring at them like they were ray guns from outer space. It was clear to me and Carl that Ronny was suffering from a deep sense of shock. He couldn't find his place.

Finally, Carl closed the door on the press — shouted at them, even — and that was that.

The next few days were strained, but okay. Now that Ronny was back, Carl said he would have to be gone more during the day for business. He had visits with lawyers, probate court, and the police, plus lots of conference calls back and forth to his office in Oregon.

That was fine. I thought having the house to

ourselves might bring the old Ronny back. Things could start to be almost normal again, even though Dad wasn't there.

Normal? That's not even funny.

Carl arranged for Ronny to get back the job he'd had in high school, as an after-hours summer custodian at our old middle school. Carl thought it might help take Ronny's mind off things. Ronny agreed. His shift was 4 p.m. to 8 p.m. three days a week. He did the first shift with no problem. It was after his second shift that something happened.

I'll try to remember as many details as I can.

That evening, Carl made supper as usual. Then he went to bed early because he had to drive to the State House in Baton Rouge in the morning. I was waiting to eat with Ronny, but he didn't come at 8:30, 9, even 9:30.

I was about to wake up Carl when the phone rang. It was the head of the custodial crew at the middle school.

"Is Ronny Stone there?" he asked gruffly.

"He's not home yet," I answered.

"Well, tell him not to come back here. Ever."

"Why? What happened?" I asked.

"Because he's crazy, that's why! Setting a fire in a classroom? Look, we gave him a job because of the accident, but your brother needs help. It's all I can do to keep the assistant principal from pressing charges —"

"Fire? What?" I asked. "Can you tell me —"

"Let him tell you!"

Click.

Ronny stumbled in around ten o'clock. The first thing I noticed was the tied-up plastic bag dangling from his wrist. Something heavy pooled at the bottom of the bag. And I could smell smoke. Not cigarettes — it was something else I couldn't identify.

"Your boss called," I said, standing. "What happened?"

"I walked out," he said.

"But I thought it was working out okay," I said. "You loved that school."

"That's what the old guy said, too, but then what are these? I thought I got rid of all of them."

I took the plastic bag and looked inside.

At the bottom were what looked like rats. Three rats, maybe four, charred black. I shoved the bag back at Ronny. "Gross! Get those out of here!"

"You've seen them before," he snapped. "It was your turn last week, so these are your fault."

"What are you talking about?"

He dropped the bag on the floor. "Besides, I couldn't stand the noise in those hallways. It made my head spin."

"What noise?" I asked. "Isn't the school mostly empty in the summer?"

Ronny slapped his hands over his ears. "The voices! It was the same as at the ravine. The stupid moaning and groaning. I just want to go home. How far is it from here, anyway? I've gotta get home."

The moaning and groaning?

"Ronny, you *are* home —"

Then, I don't know what happened. He began to mutter to himself, something about a shed and a trestle and some word that sounded like "Angola." I couldn't make any sense of his words before he finally walked out of the room.

I had to get rid of the rats. I dropped them into the garbage can outside the courtyard gate and twisted the lid tight. My blood chilled.

I couldn't sleep after that. I just stared at the ceiling of my room. Rats? What exactly had Ronny done in that school? Set rats on fire?

The next morning, I found him walking down the hall to the bathroom. He opened every door on both sides of the hallway and looked in with a blank face. He left each door open and passed on to the next one, as if he were searching for something.

"Hey, you want to do something?" I asked him.

Ronny whirled to face me. "Yeah," he said, grinning

and suddenly reminding me of his face before the accident. "Maybe we can . . . maybe we can . . ."

He drifted off, his face twisted.

"Ronny?" I asked.

He turned and walked away down the hall.

"Want to go get some comic books?" I asked.

He kept going as if he hadn't heard me. No, that's not right. He heard me, I'm sure he did. But he kept on moving as if he didn't think I was talking to *him*.

Suddenly, he faced me. "Don't you have chores to do? Get going!"

He grumbled something else, too. I couldn't make out anything except that word again: "Angola." He snarled it, like he hated the sound of it. I didn't know what it meant outside of a country in Africa, and I couldn't believe Ronny knew any kind of geography. Plus, there was another word he said with it. It sounded like "fate," or "rate," or "hate." It was all nonsense to me — *Angola fate?* — but it obviously meant something to him.

The next afternoon, Samantha came over. I told her Ronny was still "finding his way." Uncle Carl had said that once, and I couldn't think of any other way to put it. She said she understood. Ronny was sitting in the courtyard, staring into space, when I walked her out to him.

"Oh my gosh, Ronny!" Sam said, sobbing and wrapping her arms around him. He didn't budge from his position in the chair. She pulled away, surprised, and glanced at me.

"I couldn't believe it when I heard," she said quietly.

Ronny's eyes were cold. "So?"

She ignored the word and pulled up a chair next to his. I went to my room. From my window over the patio, I could hear part of their conversation.

"Sam?" he was saying, sharply. "Why do you call yourself Sam? That's a man's name."

At first I thought it was a little routine they had. She giggled to begin with, then stopped. It wasn't a routine. But Ronny kept going. "People will confuse you for a man. It's not right. Besides, I already have a sweetheart."

"Oh? Who is that?" Sam asked, straightening in her chair.

Ronny looked ready to say a name, then frowned. "No one. Forget it."

It went on like that until he finally came out with a crazy, sobbing laugh. "Get away from me! Get out!"

She bolted up from her chair. "My gosh, who *are* you?"

I saw his shoulders move. A shrug, almost like

he didn't care. Samantha left in tears through the courtyard gate. Ronny sat silent in the wicker chair. I went down to him.

When I touched his shoulder, he jumped up, whirled on his heels, and lifted his hands as if to strike me.

"What are you doing?" I backed away.

"Get away from me," he growled. He stormed into the house. His door slammed a few moments later.

For the longest time I couldn't get Sam's sobs out of my mind. I found myself asking the same question she did.

Who are *you?*

But worse was coming.

That night, I was getting ready for bed and had fallen asleep waiting for Ronny to get out of the bathroom. I woke up gasping and sweating. It was after ten, nearly eleven. I'd just had the dream again about the dogs in the bayou. I couldn't breathe. I shook my head to clear it, then slid my feet to the floor.

The carpet was damp.

I saw that the hallway floor was wet, too.

"Ronny?" I called. No answer. I went into the hall. The bathroom light was on. I saw silvery water on the wooden floor outside and heard water rushing from the faucet.

"Ronny?"

I walked quickly down the hall to the bathroom. The water was on full-blast and the bathroom sink was overflowing. I shut it off.

"Ronny, what in the world –"

He was sitting on the edge of the bathtub, rocking back and forth, clutching his left index finger with his right hand.

"What happened to you?" I asked.

"I cut myself. Shaving. I sliced my finger. It's bad."

"With the electric razor?" I said, panicking. My voice went to a scared, squeaky pitch that I'm not proud of. "How do you slice yourself with an electric razor?"

Still rocking, Ronny looked up at me. "I didn't use the electric razor. I used . . . that." He nodded to the floor under the sink.

I looked. Lying in the water was a short paring knife.

My blood went cold. "You used a kitchen knife? Are you insane? You could have killed yourself with that –"

But something else was wrong.

There was no blood.

There was only water in the sink, on the floor. Not a drop of blood. Anywhere.

"You can't have cut it that bad," I said.

"I can see the bone."

My knees weakened. "Does it hurt?"

Ronny shook his head. "No. But shouldn't it? Shouldn't it hurt a lot? It seems deep."

"Let me see it," I said.

He looked into my eyes like a lost dog, then pulled his right hand away and held the sliced finger up to me.

I jerked back. His fingertip — the top half inch or so — was gashed nearly off. When he raised his hand, the tip swung away from the rest of the finger. I felt my stomach lurch, but there was no blood coming from the wound. Glancing inside the finger, I saw nothing but pale pink "stuff" — fiber and muscle and membrane — surrounding a glimpse of white bone.

"Oh, man," I said. I felt faint.

"Is it bad?" Ronny asked innocently. "Do you think it's bad?"

I turned away, plunged my hands into the sink water, and splashed my face. I needed to shock myself out of where my stomach wanted to go.

"Tape," I said. My voice sounded hoarse, a whisper. "We have first-aid tape in the cabinet. Let's use it."

"Okay. That sounds good. Tape," Ronny said like a helpless five-year-old with a boo-boo. I dug out a roll of tape and cut off a strip with the bathroom scissors. Together, Ronny and I set his fingertip back into place and wrapped the tape around it tightly.

He held up his bandaged finger and nodded. "This is good. Thanks, brother."

I nodded. "Tomorrow we should go to the doctor —"

"You *are* my brother, right?" Ronny interrupted. His eyes searched me for an answer. "You've said so before."

Then he stood up and splashed awkwardly out of the bathroom, turning in the doorway. "How far away am I?"

"How far away? From where?" This was too weird.

"From home. By train. How far?"

"But you're —"

"Doesn't matter," he snapped, disappearing down the hall.

Twenty-eight minutes later, after I had mopped up the mess and run the incident over in my mind, I heard Ronny leave his room, walk down the stairs, open the front door, and walk out. It was his first time out of the house since he quit his job.

I decided to follow him.

EIGHT

Club Noir

It was late now, almost midnight. The sky was blackish purple, but the streets were still warm. In minutes, I was sweating under my arms, down my neck.

Why was I following him?

I didn't know. I didn't have any idea what I was doing. All I knew was that Ronny was scary, he was acting crazy, he was off . . . and he was all I had left. He had come back from the brink of death, who knows how, and he was having trouble. There was something wrong with him, but he was my brother. So I followed him.

Ronny walked a few blocks west, paused at a corner, looked around and turned north, like he just then decided where he was going. I came to the same corner and saw him walking slowly up Toulouse Street. He stopped in front of a sliver of a storefront and puzzled at the sign above the door, moving his head one way and another as if trying to read

Russian. Finally, he stepped through the door into the darkness.

I moved closer. It was a music club, one of dozens on the street. I made my way there, careful not to be seen in case Ronny came right out again. He didn't.

The name of the place was Club Noir. A black doorway gaped. No light came from inside. There were no people crowded outside as there would have been if it were open, but I heard electric guitar strings being pinched and poked. The sound reminded me how much my father loved New Orleans blues. He had dozens of recordings from local clubs. But never mind.

I crept up to the door and listened. The guitar stopped, and there was low talking I couldn't make out, then quiet. The guitar started again. It was a song. A gruff old voice joined in.

The words he sang were garbled, but I recognized one of them.

Angola.

My nerves went electric.

A half hour later, I slunk into another storefront when Ronny came out of Club Noir, wiping his face and retracing his steps south. Was he crying? I watched him walk to the corner and turn onto our street. He was going back home.

I wasn't. I went inside.

The club was as humid as a rainstorm. Two electric fans whirred across the room, but they didn't move any cool air. Instead, they blew around the smell of warm rubber that I knew came from an overheated guitar amplifier.

Seated on a low stool next to the amp was a dark giant with grizzled hair. He must have been eighty, huddled over an electric guitar that, on him, looked no bigger than a ukulele.

He was wiping his face on the shoulder of his T-shirt. Had he and Ronny been crying together? What was going on? Just as I wondered whether to bolt out of there, he looked up.

"A little past your bedtime, isn't it?" he said in a low voice.

"My name is Derek Stone," I said.

Without responding, he went at the beat-up guitar in his lap, pinching its strings. They squealed under his fingers. Twisting the final note of his run back and forth — *eee-ooo-eee-ooo* — he held it, held it, then slid his fingers off the fret board. They fell into his lap.

"I'm Bob Lemon," he said. It was the lowest voice I had ever heard, and mellow, like the purr of a racing car. "Called Big Bob Lemon, mostly." His hand, when he extended it, was as large as a baseball mitt. I felt like a tiny ball of fresh mozzarella next to him.

"What can I do for you?" he went on. He looked at me with his head angled, and I realized that his right eye was false. I tried not to look at it.

I weighed what to say. "Look, sir, I don't know why I came, actually. I don't know. But I just saw my brother come in here. He's been having problems. . . ."

Big Bob Lemon shook his head slowly. He set his hands on the guitar again, then took them off without playing a note. He was silent for a very long minute.

"That boy is not your brother."

I laughed nervously. "You're kidding, right?"

He went back to playing. It was up to me to keep the conversation going.

"He's my brother. I followed him from our house."

"No, he's not," the man said, stopping again. "That boy may look like your brother. Talk like him, even. But it isn't him. It isn't him just like a ghost isn't a person."

I couldn't help it — I shivered. "A ghost? What are you talking about?"

"Think about it," Lemon went on. "Has he been acting like your brother? Like the brother you knew growing up?"

That stopped me. How did *he* know?

"He just came back from a terrible accident," I said.

"You sure it's your brother who came back?"

I felt my chest tighten as I got annoyed. "I don't know what you're talking about. You have no idea what he's been through."

"He was in the train that fell at Bordelon," he said.

I swallowed. "Right."

"So were you," he added. "Are *you* okay?"

"Me?"

"You were in the crash."

"So?"

"So you're you, but he's not him," Lemon said matter-of-factly, like it actually made sense. "And that's not his house you followed him from. Not anymore. He's somebody else now. I know him, but you don't."

I shook my head. "What are you talking about? *You* know him?"

"That is, I saw him before, only he didn't look like that."

My ear twinged sharply. "This is nuts —"

"Look, *he* came here," the man said. "He found me here because he knows me. He helped me once when I was a young boy, riding the rails. And he needed to talk about that."

I looked at Big Bob Lemon. "Ronny helped you when you were a young boy? Yeah. Right. I need to get out of here."

Lemon stood up. He towered over me, but his voice was still quiet and low. "What you need to do is follow him. You need to listen to him. Find out what you can. He may not be your brother anymore, but he's somebody. And he sure as day needs you."

None of that made any sense to me. Nothing made sense anymore.

"I heard you sing something about 'Angola,'" I said, changing the subject. "What does that mean?"

"Country in Africa, is all I know," Big Bob replied curtly. "Of course, you could look it up. You might find something different."

He sat down and started playing his guitar again. That was it. Conversation over.

NINE

I Am Not Alone

I stepped onto the street and walked to the corner. It was very late now. The first neon signs were going off. From pink, blue, orange, red, the street was turning gray. *The trembling time,* I thought, though I couldn't tell you why I thought that or where those words came from.

I walked on. Stopped.

Are *you* okay?

Uh-huh. Yeah. You're a nut, old man, that's all —

Then I heard the deep voices again.

They came in waves, an incoming, outgoing tide of low anguished moaning, reaching toward me from the darkness, then pulling back. It must have looked weird to anyone who saw me tilting my head this way and that like a dog listening for its master's call. It would have looked weird, except there wasn't anyone to see me.

The street was empty.

When I turned the corner onto Royal Street, my

spine tingled up to my neck and into my bad ear. Whatever was making the sound had moved, too. Just not at the same pace I was moving. Sometimes it was closer, sometimes farther away. It was always the same tone, always echoing as if it came from some low place, a crypt or an underground chamber, out of the *damp-stone, stone-cold, cold-dead room*.

More words? Now I was really freaking myself out.

I hurried toward an arcade on the other side of the street and turned right, plowing into a group of tourists gawking at a menu outside an all-night café.

"Sorry," I said, hurrying on.

The voices got louder again. Was I crazy? I zigzagged across the next street and tore through the first open shop I saw, the twenty-four hour bookstore near my house, hoping for a clear path from front to back. No such luck. I had to weave between bookcases and spinning racks.

"Hey, kid," the cashier called. Her frown shot daggers. "Slow down!"

Several people spun around as I hustled to the back door. It was half open because someone had just come in. I barreled past her, spitting out an apology. "Sorry —"

"Jerk!" an older girl said.

Maybe the voices had been drowned out by the too-loud music in the store. Maybe it was the quiet of the back street. But the moment I stepped outside, the voices rushed at me again. They were following me.

But what *were* they? Dad's mother had heard songs before she died. Great, now I was acting like an eighty-year-old. Was it genetic? Had I really gotten messed up in the accident? My left ear was killing me. It felt like a long needle was slowly being pushed . . .

I ran to the end of the alley, froze, turned my head.

Could no one else hear the voices?

Are *you* okay?

I ran back into the bookstore.

"You again?" shouted the cashier. "See if I don't call the police on you —"

"Please don't," I said, heading for the front of the store again, when something went *snap* in my mind. The voices stopped. Just like that.

I froze next to a display table, holding it to steady myself. I listened. Nothing. No voices.

I looked around, my eyes finally focusing, and I saw books. Hundreds of books. History. Science. Technology.

Books.

They gave me an idea I should have had before.

"I'm dialing! Nine . . . one . . ." the cashier called out.

I couldn't say whether or not the voices were really gone. All I knew was that I needed to get home.

TEN

The Oak Panel

My shirt was completely soaked by the time I slid into the house and locked the door behind me. I thought I'd locked it quietly, but Carl was on me in a second. He shuffled in quickly from the living room, angry with me for being out so late without calling. He had to drive first thing in the morning. Then he stopped, he just shut it off, and looked at me like Dad used to. Concerned.

"Is everything all right, Derek?"

Big Bob Lemon's voice echoed in my head. *Are you okay?* "Why?"

"Well, it's your face. Like you've seen . . . you're really pale."

"I'm okay," I said.

"Yeah?"

"Yeah. Sure."

Carl shooed me toward the stairs, but I said I needed a snack before bed and told him to go on up.

"Turn off the lights," he said, yawning as he climbed the stairs. "I'm glad you're all right." After his door clicked closed, I stood in the front hall, listening for a few minutes. Nothing. I took off my shoes and went upstairs.

The voices came back again, rumbling below everything, but they were outside now. Or somewhere else, anyway. I could still only hear them in my left ear. It sounded like the earbud of my iPod had fallen out of my right ear. Whatever. Maybe it was just the rumble of the city. Or maybe I was overly tired.

Ronny was asleep on his bed when I passed his room. His face was hard, frowning, even in sleep.

He looked confused. Or lost.

Ideas about what was going on swarmed in my mind, but none of them made sense.

How could Ronny actually be alive? I saw him fly out the train window. But how could he be dead for a month, and now suddenly not be? Why had he trapped and killed those rats? Why was he so mean to Sam? Why had he gone to Club Noir? How did he know Big Bob Lemon? What was "Angola"? *Look it up,* the man told me. *That boy is not your brother,* he told me. *Just like a ghost isn't a person,* he said.

And ghosts? No. No way. Never. That's fantasy. That's unreal. You hear a lot about ghosts in New

Orleans, with its long haunted history, cold houses, wispy apparitions. They were no more than dry floorboards and loose windows and fog.

I hated it, all of it. I had to know real information. Solid stuff. And now I knew where to start.

I crept quietly up to the third floor, to my father's office, and searched his desk. There were bills and maintenance reports, mortgage documents, receipts, estimates, scraps of paper scrawled with telephone messages or random numbers. Carl had arranged them in piles and was obviously dealing with them as best he could.

There was nothing there that could help me. I expected that. I knew where I would end up. But first, I booted up Dad's computer and did a search on the word "Angola."

Beyond the listings for the country in Africa, there were a few about Angola, Louisiana — where the main state prison was.

The state prison. I didn't know what to make of that.

Then I searched for Big Bob Lemon and came up with a brief encyclopedia entry on his career as a musician. It said that he was born in 1929 and lost an eye in an accident — a train accident — when he was nine.

Which would have been in 1938.

Huh.

I searched train accidents in 1938. All I found was a short list of book titles, most of them histories of railroading in Louisiana. I jotted down the titles. I had to move on.

I turned off the desk light and stood in the hall outside the office. From there, I could see a narrow set of plain oak stairs at the end of the hall. The lower steps were lit, while the upper ones lay in shadow, indistinct. I knew where the steps led. To the *faux chambre*. The fake room.

Only it wasn't fake, was it? It was Dad's private room, where he kept his trains and books. I had never been up there before. Not really because I respected Dad's privacy. No, it was more that I just didn't care. Old train models? Eh.

I headed up the stairs. There was no door at the top. Instead, I faced a wall of burnished oak panels. The central panel was narrow, but it went from ceiling to floor and was tall, almost like a pantry door. It was the most logical entrance to the room beyond, so I pushed.

Nothing.

I felt around the panel, trying to nudge it from side to side. It shifted slightly, though it seemed heavier than I expected and was more solidly built than I could have imagined. Following the edge of the panel with my fingers, I pushed, pulled, pressed all the way around. The seam between the panel and the frame made a slight cracking sound. Then I realized it didn't push in or pull out like a door at all. It dipped in and slid aside, disappearing into a space in the doorframe.

"A pocket door," I said softly.

When I moved the panel aside, a wave of stale air flowed over me. I crawled through the opening and stepped inside. The room was small, but not as small as it looked from the street.

A large desk and chair occupied the center of the room. Above and below the windows on the eight walls were bookcases; the uppermost shelf ran unbroken around the room and had a track on it that was filled with model trains. The ceiling of the octagonal room was made of eight panels sloping up to a point in the center, which I knew was directly under the gilt angel you could see from the street.

When I slid the door closed — *snap!* — the voices, distant as they were, were sheared off completely. It was quiet. I felt safe in a way I hadn't since the accident. I cracked a window, breathed in the night air over the city. Still no voices. Strange.

It was a handsome little room. And there were books. Hundreds of them. Louisiana history. Railroads. Locomotives. Engineering books. Geography books. Atlases. Labor history. It was running through the bookstore that had given me the idea to come up here in the first place. Dad had so many books that I'd had no interest in — until now.

With the list of book titles from the Internet in hand, I rummaged through Dad's shelves. His collection was arranged alphabetically by author, and I soon found two books on the list and three others that might help. I sat at his desk and first flipped to the indexes. My hands shook when I saw an entry for the term, "Angola Freight."

"What —?"

I turned to the page listed and found that "Angola Freight" was what they called the train that carried convicts to the penitentiary in Angola. The "freight" referred to was, of course, prisoners.

As I read further, my hands shook.

On the night of June 3, 1938, a bridge on the rail line between Alexandria and Angola collapsed. A train carrying prisoners crashed into Bordelon Gap.

"Are you kidding me?" I said aloud. I couldn't help talking to myself. What difference did it make? I'd already been acting completely nuts.

I scanned the next ten pages without seeing anything more about the crash. The next books had no other information about Angola Freight or the 1938 crash, either. Two of them did refer to the same article in a small newspaper called the *Marksville Ledger*, which seemed like it might have the most details of the crash.

I closed the last book, got up, and paced the room from window to window. I could see the floodlights around the cemetery and the glimmering water, the cemetery, the water, cemetery, water, as I tried to understand what I'd just read.

The desk lamp, dim as it was, shed an orangey-gold light in the room. The shelves holding Dad's collection of trains looked like they were burning.

I found myself peering at the center of the ceiling as I turned off the light. When I slid the door back in place, the voices, though faraway and disjointed, began again.

My sense of safety disappeared.

Books in hand, I went back down to Dad's office and searched the public library database on his computer. My heart leaped. Issues of the *Marksville Ledger* were in the main collection.

"Tomorrow," I muttered to myself. "Early."

Lying in bed a few minutes later, I stared at the ceiling. As I imagined the gold angel flying above me in the black sky, I realized that something had changed. I had something to do. And it was real.

Maybe it wouldn't make Ronny be himself again, and maybe it wouldn't bring Dad home, but it was the first real thing I'd be doing since the accident.

At the very least, I was going to find out *something*.

But I had no idea what.

ELEVEN

Fears

When nine o'clock rolled around the next morning, I headed to the main library, a streetcar ride and a short walk away on Loyola Street.

It was a gray day, not too hot, but I was already sweating. I wasn't fully awake, either. Still, it felt good to be going to gather information, comforting, like a defense, like building a kind of armor. It would be a long road, and I was just beginning, but I was heading in the right direction.

I could just tell.

A young guy sat behind the library's periodicals desk with a fan blowing in his face. He had a beard that looked like dirt, but he smiled when I walked in. I showed him my library card.

"Whoa, you're the guy whose brother died and then didn't, huh?" he asked.

"That's me," I said, unfazed. I told him what I wanted. He tapped away on his keyboard, shook his head, frowned, then looked up.

"The *Marksville Ledger* isn't digital," he said.

"Okay . . ."

"And the microfilm is stored up in the State House. But we have the original newspapers."

"Can I see them?" I asked.

"Not here," he said. "They're in the annex on Marais Street. Behind Armstrong Park."

I calculated the distance in my head. "Can I go there? I mean, is it open? Will they let me in?"

"Yes, yes, and yes," the guy said, pleased with himself for being able to answer that way. "I'll call and tell them you're coming. Not many people go there, so they have to open the collection especially for you. But that's what they get paid for, so, you know . . ."

"Thanks a lot," I said.

It was near ten now, and the morning was still gray, though hotter. I sweated more, walking through the open park to the buildings beyond.

Library annex? I thought for sure the guy was sending me to a trailer with lightbulbs hanging from the ceiling. He wasn't. The annex was a big old marble building, a former bank in the heart of a neighborhood that time had passed by.

I pulled the door open. An older woman sat behind a metal desk, looking drowsy. She jerked up when the door squeaked.

I looked past her, deep into a palace of dust. There must have been hundreds of stacks of moldy records, handwritten documents, deeds, crumbling books, thick old ledgers, brown newspapers, personal archives, one-of-a-kind publications, paper, paper, paper. It was like a scene out of Dickens.

The lady rang a bell, and something in the dark end of a hallway to my right began to creak toward me. I wanted to run, but the lady showed no signs of fear, so I tried not to, either. What seemed like hours later, an untucked old attendant with a jowly, unshaven face emerged, limping across the floorboards to the desk. He smelled like charred coffee and mothballs.

I half-expected him to speak in some unintelligible language, but he didn't say a word. He only turned away and ushered me wordlessly down another corridor and a steep set of stairs, to an underground series of rooms. Stack after stack, shelf after shelf, I felt like I was moving backward through time.

I didn't like the feeling.

The old guy slumped in a chair, huffing out a great musty breath. Still saying nothing, he pointed across the room to the shelves and shelves of newspapers. I started in on them. After a while, I dug up issues of the *Marksville Ledger*. I found the article about the accident on the first page of a paper dated June 5, 1938, two days after the first train tumbled into Bordelon Gap.

I wiped a layer of dust off the reading table, sat, and began to read. The details of the crash were eerily similar to mine. Most of the convict train's cars made it across the bridge, when stress on the rails caused the bridge to buckle. The end car went sliding into the ravine, resulting in seventeen fatalities.

"Trestles snapped . . . car fell backward . . . struck the ravine's deep slope . . . buckled . . . fire . . ."

The very same.

There was a grainy photo of the river twisting below the crash site, looking the same as when I had been there. My eyes closed and I saw it again, churning like a black snake. *River of many deaths.*

I read that not everyone killed in the 1938 crash was a criminal. There was a woman, the wife of a convict who was accompanying her husband, an arsonist, to jail. They let her on the train because he was going to be executed. She was ill and probably wouldn't live to see her husband again. Two guards also died in the crash. One was trapped in the wreck and killed in the fire. The other man, a young guard on his first day at work, was thrown from the car as it broke in half.

Broke in half? What a first day.

That's when I read something that freaked me out entirely. The young guard was a guy named Virgil Black who came from a little town called Shongaloo, but the name of the older guard was Jubal Higgins.

Jubal Higgins!

Ronny had said that. He'd said, *Daddy Jubal*. What did it mean?

There was more.

Among the survivors was "a Negro boy aged nine, Robert Lemon, who suffered head injuries and possible blindness."

"What!" I slapped the paper down on the table and stood up. "Big Bob Lemon, who was nine years old in 1938? Is this seriously saying that Big Bob Lemon is the boy from the crash? How did Ronny know?"

"Shhh," said the attendant, who had woken up.

Fine. Fine. But how could Ronny possibly know about *any* of this? Angola Freight? Daddy Jubal? As Tooley had said, Ronny was the last person to read history books or use a computer to find information. Where did he get these facts? And why was he talking to strangers about this?

Or *was* he a stranger to Big Bob Lemon?

Lemon had said that Ronny was someone else. He'd said he *knew* Ronny. That he helped him when he was a young boy riding the rails.

What! What! What!

I didn't believe — I *couldn't* believe — where my mind was taking me. But what exactly were the facts?

Two trains crashed in the same place.

Ronny survived but was acting weird, saying and doing things that weren't like him.

He talked about the Angola Freight.

He talked to a victim of the first crash.

I read and reread the article a dozen times, then finally photocopied it, left, and walked back through the park to the main library. I collected a bunch of geography and travel books, and found a secluded table near the stairs on the top floor. It felt better to be up high, and I was near the stairs in case I heard more weird voices.

Thumbing through the books, I read about how Bordelon Gap was a ravine between two halves of a low mountain. The river running through the Gap was part of the Red River, which ran across the entire state from northwest to southeast. It was nearly inaccessible from the Gap, and treacherous because of its rapids and the speed of its current.

I read as much as I could, until there was no more to read. Not in that section of the library, at least. Unable to stop myself, I edged into the stacks on

Louisiana legends. Ghost stories. I couldn't believe I was doing this.

I scanned shelves of books on the paranormal. Stories about hauntings. Doctored photographs. I flipped through them, my stomach turning with each page. It was all so . . . made up! I hated that kind of book. Bogus history. Wishful thinking. Hocus-pocus! And yet, before slamming the books shut I checked every table of contents, endnote, and index. I wrote down what I read about auditory manifestations, apparitions, hauntings, spiritual places.

When I stopped for a minute, I realized that I was breathing heavily. I thought about all the things Ronny had done since he came back. One after another, they piled up and scared the life out of me. It terrified me to think of it: Ronny didn't know me, he wasn't himself, he wasn't the brother I'd had for fourteen years. He was . . . *someone else*.

Finally, it was a book called *Afterlives* by a man named Tomas Deak that stopped me cold. It said the usual weirdness about why things like ghosts actually exist. I was about to toss it aside with the others when I came upon what the author said could happen at the exact moment of death.

The movement of souls — from one body to another.

TWELVE

Gobbledygook?

Lunchtime came and went while I read the book from cover to cover.

The movement of souls.

It sounded horrific and impossible and insane and wrong.

But I forced myself to read it. Through page after page, my shoulders and neck felt besieged by tiny spiders. My legs turned to ice. I breathed the shallowest breaths.

The book basically argued that when a body dies, its soul moves off, leaving the dead form and going to some kind of afterlife. Most people believe something like that happens, and then it's over.

Except maybe it's not over.

Not always.

For the tiniest fraction of the brief moment of death — like the time between, say, Tuesday and Wednesday — the place the soul vacates is left open like a kind of vacuum. In that moment, a second soul — one that's been waiting — can enter and reanimate that dead body. The body "lives" again with a different soul.

Do you understand what I'm telling you here? Some people actually believe that at the instant of death, a long-dead soul can trade places with a dying soul.

And the dead soul lives again.

Not as a ghost, no. Something worse.

I thought of zombies, the walking dead, but that wasn't right, either. Another soul was in the body now.

It made me think of a kind of translation from one body to another.

Translation.

Impossible?

Absolutely . . . right?

The author, who was an anatomist, took it even further. He theorized that two souls could probably only exchange places if their causes of death were identical. The two bodies had to arrive at the moment of death the very same way, or it wouldn't work. That's why it was so rare.

Rare. But not impossible. The accident Ronny, Dad, and I were in was nearly identical to the 1938 accident at the same place.

I didn't want to keep reading, but I couldn't stop myself.

The author went on to say that some people believe the worlds of the living and the dead exist side by side, separated only by a kind of fabric. There are texts going back thousands of years about this division of worlds. Spirits are immaterial, they have no solid form, so they can slip back and forth between the worlds. They can haunt us if they want to.

Fine. That's ghosts.

But what if sometime, somehow, the fabric is torn? What if it actually gets a rip in it? Why and how this might happen nobody knows, but if it did, a dead soul — the part of a person that never really dies — might escape from the afterlife through the tear and translate into a dying body.

Making it live again.

Making it live again?

I wanted to stomp on that book and throw it out the window. I wanted to scream and run out of that stupid library and never come back. But I didn't move.

I remembered the nauseous sense of free fall on the train. My father's coiling scream. Ronny's flight through the window. The jagged ravine. I knew that if I let myself, I would imagine the wreck over and over and not be able to stop.

I stood up. If I believed the book, I'd have to believe that dead souls were waiting in the Bordelon Gap, waiting for a second train to crash right where theirs did. I tried to imagine a tear in the fabric separating life and death. I tried to imagine the souls of the dead crowded at the opening like captives at a door to freedom. When the train fell and people died, the circumstances were exactly the same as the crash in 1938. Dead souls escaped the afterlife and translated into the dying bodies.

So the book was asking me to believe that inside Ronny was someone who died in the first train wreck, that my brother was dead, but that his body was now inhabited by someone else? But who?

I searched the photocopy of the newspaper. Virgil Black. The young guard.

The idea of a long-dead soul entering a just-dead body made me sick with horror. It sounded repulsive and painful. I tried to swallow, tried to breathe, when all of a sudden – *bang!* – the stair door flew open and Ronny charged at me.

"You!" he cried.

I fell back into my chair. "How – how did you know to look for me here?"

His expression was like a madman's. Was he in pain? His hair was wild, his eyes bloodshot. He stormed up and down the stacks, his head turning madly from side to side.

A security guard edged through the stacks toward us. He was reaching for his walkie-talkie.

"We're fine, sir," I said. "Ronny, outside. Outside."

We hurried down the stairs to the square outside the library. It was hot, the sun burning behind the haze. A crowd had gathered to listen to a couple playing a violin and a banjo badly. I pulled Ronny into the shadows of a nearby arcade.

"What's wrong?" I asked.

"What's happening to me?" he groaned. "I feel like I'm being taken over. I don't know what's going on in my head —"

"Ronny, cool down," I said. My heart thundered.

"This is insanity. That's what this is. I'm going crazy. I don't know who I am anymore. I never should have left Shongaloo. That's when it all went wrong —"

"Have left *where*?" I said.

Without warning, he bolted down the arcade toward the street.

I tore the photocopied article out of my pocket. My eyes could hardly focus, but I strained to read it, and there was the word — Shongaloo. It was the young prison guard's hometown. I read his name again. Then I heard deep voices. Moaning.

Ronny stopped running and walked back to me, his eyes pleading. "You hear them, too?"

"I . . . think I do," I said. "Don't ask me how . . ."

He slapped his hands on my shoulders, his eyes welling with tears. "You don't know what this means! You hear them, too! The voices are getting closer all the time. They've come back —"

I shivered. "Who? Who are they? Ronny, look. We should go home. There's something I need to show you —"

His face turned dark. "This isn't my home. I — I have to get out. I have to go —"

He tried to twist out of my grip.

"Don't leave," I said, holding on to his cold wrist.

"I had to leave you!" he snarled. "I had to get a job to help Momma. I had to — let go of me!" He jerked his arm away and stomped down the arcade toward the street.

"Wait," I said. "Wait . . . Virgil . . ."

THIRTEEN

The Past Is Not Past

Ronny froze in his tracks. He was still Ronny to me, even if he . . . wasn't. He turned slowly back to face me. "What did you call me?"

"Vir — Virgil," I said softly, stumbling over the name I dreaded saying. "Virgil Black . . ."

Color flushed his cheeks. "You know me?"

So it was true.

I pulled him to a bench under the arcade.

"How can you know me . . . ?" he asked.

"Look," I said as calmly as I could, trying to settle myself as much as him. "Maybe I do. Maybe I don't. Never mind that now. You need to tell me what you remember. About before."

Ronny's eyes darted around. "What? Before?"

I couldn't believe my own words. "Before the train wreck. What do you remember?"

He made a sound in his throat like gagging, then rolled his palms into his temples. His face twisted in pain. He clenched his eyes shut. When he opened them, they stared blankly into the distance.

"It was my first job after leaving home," he said. "My first day. I had been hired as a guard. I came from Shongaloo. I caught vermin, rats, mice in the barns. Just like I taught you . . . or someone, maybe not you. This was my first real job. Momma cried the day I left."

It was hard to believe I was hearing this. It proved just how close those thoughts were to him, wherever they came from.

"Go on."

"We were putting them on the train, helping them up the steps."

"Helping who?" I asked.

"It's hard to get up the steps with the ankle bracelets they wore."

"Who did? What steps?"

"The convicts, up the steps into the train car. Me and Daddy Jubal helped them. He was head guard that day."

It was like listening to an old man remember his long-ago youth, except I was looking at a nineteen-year-old boy. It was Ronny, only it wasn't. It wasn't even his voice anymore. It was lower, thicker.

"Of course, I was mighty scared," he went on.

"Why?"

"Because of Erskine Cane. He was the main one we were transporting that day. He was out of his mind. A killer. He had this crazy smile on his face. It had been there since I first saw him, and it wouldn't leave. Didn't matter that he was going to Angola to die. Didn't mean a thing to him. He was a big man, and strong. Convicted of burning houses for fun. Three families died before he was caught. He was going to prison to be executed."

I remembered the newspapers in the library annex. "There was a woman, too, right?"

Ronny nodded. "His wife. As loony as he was. No smile, though. A face like a corpse. She was crazy and dying, and looked more than halfway there —"

He froze. A streetcar traveled slowly past the square where we sat. Ronny shivered and looked away.

"And the accident?" I asked quietly. I didn't want to hear it, but I had to.

He described it just as the old newspaper had. It sounded almost exactly the same as the collapse we — Ronny and I — had gone through together.

"I was thrown from the window of the train car. I saw it explode. I fell hard. There was a boy I tried to help . . . he was bleeding, I moved him . . ."

"He was nine," I whispered. "Bob Lemon."

He rocked back and forth on the bench, nodding. "Then I lost my footing and fell into the chasm . . . onto the rocks . . . the rocks was where . . ." He stopped.

I couldn't imagine it, the horror of it. "And after that?"

He searched my face. "*After* that?"

"When you were . . . in the ravine."

Ronny shut his eyes again and rubbed his temples. "I can't . . . see it."

The voices rang in my head suddenly. I bolted up. He did, too.

"You hear them again?" he asked.

"I shouldn't be able to, right?" I said, pressing my ear closed. "I survived the accident."

"I don't know," he said.

The voices rolled and twisted over one another.

"Who are they?" I asked, wincing.

"I don't know," Ronny said again. "The dead?"

I snorted a laugh. "Boy, we're a couple of people who don't know a lot, aren't we?"

I thought I saw a hint of a smile. "I don't know. I don't know anything."

I looked into his eyes then and felt as if we had broken through a wall and were together again, Ronny and me. Only it wasn't Ronny anymore.

It was someone named Virgil.

"We have to go back to the bridge," I said. "You have to see it, to remember what happened there. And we need to find out what we can about our . . . my . . . dad."

"You mean, maybe he's alive?"

"He could still be there, hurt," I said.

He searched my eyes. "Bordelon Gap?"

"Bordelon Gap."

He nodded slowly. "I'll drive."

FOURTEEN

Dark River

So, was that it?

I didn't fight it anymore? Had I accepted that Ronny was . . . gone? And did I really believe that in his place was someone else, someone who died seventy years ago, someone named Virgil Black?

I don't know what to tell you.

I don't know what to tell you, except that I had driven with Ronny lots of times, and no way was my brother behind the wheel on the way to Bordelon Gap. It was amazing that Virgil Black hadn't died in a car crash long before he ever got on that convict train. For him, a steering wheel was a deadly weapon.

Those crazy cop chases on TV had nothing on this guy.

"Hoo-wee!" he yelled like the farm boy he used to be. "I started driving when I was thirteen, but this . . . *this*!"

He didn't seem to care about speed limits or stop

signs. He drove into every pothole as if he was aiming at it. He cut people off. He never used his turn signal. He drove completely off the road and careened back onto sidewalks, over lawns, between light poles.

When we reached Bordelon Gap, I stumbled out of the car, feeling like I'd just survived a five-hour roller-coaster ride with a madman.

"Never drove on real roads much, did you?" I asked him.

Ronny grinned. "Nope. But I will now!"

It was good — really good — to joke with him, like old times. But as soon as he caught sight of the chasm and the river below, his flash of humor was gone.

I was alone with a dead man again.

"Let's get closer," he said.

Giant trucks blocked the rails on both sides of the fallen bridge. The whole area was crawling with police and construction crews. The rescue work was done; now they were rebuilding the bridge. Men in yellow hard hats were scouring the site, picking up debris.

The ravine was steep all the way to the bottom. My legs turned to jelly when I peered down at the black water, and I thought of those words again.

Dark river, rolling river, river of many deaths. I couldn't imagine anyone coming up out of that.

And then the terror of water fell over me. That was it, wasn't it? I saw water and my own nightmare returned.

I was looking down Bordelon Gap, but all I could see was the place I'd tried so hard to forget.

Bayou Malpierre.

I was young, barely four years old. For some reason I've tried hard to remember but can't, I was walking in a bayou thick with trees that arched over black water. It was nearly night and hot and raining. Who was I with? I don't know. Darkness fell quickly. I got separated.

There I was, a little boy lost among the dark trees, the moss and the stink of vegetation and the slow black water and the rain. I remember calling out, but softly. I didn't want to wake the ghosts I thought lived in the water.

And the rain came down harder.

I whispered for help. How dumb was that? I whispered for help, so of course, no one heard me. With every moment, I was becoming more lost, trying to find my way through the dense trees.

Then there were the dogs. Five, six, seven, barking and squealing and wailing in the close, soggy growth around me. Not search dogs. Wild dogs, bayou dogs. They smelled my fear. They were gathering and howling and coming closer. I heard their paws sloshing in the water. Eerie keening, echoing in the swampy darkness.

Gasping for air, stone-cold frightened, I ran over the soft ground. Reeds whipped my face.

Then there were stones. Headstones. Where was I? A cemetery? In the bayou?

I slipped on the spongy ground, struck the back of my head on a stone, slid into the black water. I tried to pull myself up, but the rain pounded me down. The swamp was deep. Hands and old dead faces gathered around me in the rank water, drawing me to them.

And the dogs came closer, closer. Water covered my face, went into my mouth, my nose. I tried to scream. I swallowed mouthfuls of the foul black liquid.

Suddenly, there was a popping sound. Gunshots. Dogs wailed and howled and something — a hand — reached through the water for me. Warm and strong. I was heaved back up onto land. Pressure on my chest, lungs bursting, someone else's air in my mouth and throat.

I screamed water.

I remember my whole body heaving, swallowing air. Then I was alone.

I was four years old. Alone in a bayou. Why was I there? Who had saved me? Who had run the dogs off, pulled me out of the dark swamp, given me his breath?

No one would talk about it. Dad said no, it wasn't him, that maybe I dreamed the whole thing. Why would a four-year-old be alone in the bayou?

I asked Mom once. We were on a narrow street, buildings all around. She touched my damaged ear, claimed maybe I saw a movie — she named two or three I could have glimpsed some scenes of and might be remembering. She left for France soon after. Ronny said that if it did happen like I said, it must have been when he was away at a swim meet. But he was nine when it happened. He wasn't swimming in meets yet.

No one believed me.

Bzzzz! I was near the crest of the chasm, looking down, shivering, when my pocket hummed. *Bzzzz!*

A policeman turned at the sound. Ronny pulled me down behind a rock. "What's that?"

"Cell phone," I whispered. "Sorry —"

"Make it shut up!" he hissed.

I plunged my hand into my pocket and switched the phone off. We couldn't be spotted. We weren't supposed to be there. I looked up.

The officer scanned the hill. He turned back to

talk to a man in a gray jumpsuit, who removed his hard hat and mopped his forehead with a gloved hand.

Ronny was frowning something fierce. His eyes were fixed on the twisting river at the bottom of the ravine.

I tugged on his sleeve. "Come on, Ronny. We need to back away."

He didn't move.

I hated to do it, but I said his other name again. "Virgil . . ."

He stared down at the water, his forehead furrowing.

"Darkness," he said finally. "For a long time, there was only darkness. It felt like I was floating, swimming in nothing. For years. For a long time."

"You remember that?" I said, feeling cold all of a sudden.

Ronny sucked in a huge breath, said nothing.

"Then what?" I asked.

"Others," he said. "Others were with me. I can feel them even now, hear them whisper, sense them doing that thing they do instead of breathing. It's like moaning. Voices without bodies."

"Who are they?" I asked.

"Daddy Jubal. The others. The mad wife. They're . . . angry. Fighting."

His face went icy white. His eyelids flickered. "We were crowded at the door. Only it wasn't a door. It was like . . . a gash, ripped across the air. There was a tear of light, sudden, from top to bottom. And water. We all started to rise to it."

What Ronny was talking about wasn't the great white light you see near death. This was something else. Torn fabric, the opening between the worlds. The souls of the dead were crowded at it — waiting to cross over.

Ronny rubbed his eyes. "In the light, I saw a train swimming down through the air. Like the accident that killed me, only it wasn't me this time. It was someone else falling. Something pushed me toward the opening. I could see the falling boy, hear his cries as he fell onto the rocks. I swept up out of the water and went to him. Then I . . . I . . . I was that boy, falling into the river, going under until I stopped. There was a crook in the river, a bank that arched out, holding me safe like an arm. Hours passed, days passed. I am the boy now."

The full realization of what I had read now stabbed its way into my head. He was talking about dead souls. He was talking about translation.

"It was Ronny," I said.

He turned. "You call me that."

I wanted to cry.

"The others came with me through the opening," he went on. "*He* was there. The big, dark shape, like an ox. I'm afraid of him."

A siren whirred on the slope above us. I pulled Ronny's head lower.

"Do they see us?" he asked.

"Not yet," I said. "Who are you afraid of?"

"Cane," he whispered. "Erskine Cane, the arsonist. The killer. He came back, too. He . . . wants something here."

Ronny paused, still staring at the water below. "They're here. I feel their pain, the pain of being here again. I hear their voices. You do, too."

But why, I wondered. Why?

"They know I'm here," he said. "They know I know about them."

Did they know about me, too? How could they?

I survived the accident.

I never died.

I wanted to say it was insane, but I couldn't form the words, not even in my head. He was talking about the torn fabric and about translation. Virgil Black, long-dead victim of the first bridge collapse, was telling me how he looked out from the world of the dead, saw Ronny die the same way he had, and took his place.

So that's it, then.

Translation happens.

"You there!" yelled a voice. I looked up. The police officer was edging quickly down the hillside.

"What are you two doing?" he shouted. Sirens wailed.

"Dang," said Ronny, watching a black-and-white cruiser roar up over the crest. Another. A third.

He ran along the ledge, then stopped in his tracks. His face twisted. He slapped a hand over one ear.

"What's the matter?" I asked. "Come on —"

"Quiet!" he snapped. His body tensed as if he was ready to fight. "Oh, no . . ." He turned and scanned the ravine.

I saw them at the same time he did, a little below us. Two men.

One was short and wiry, like a greyhound in a dark uniform. He stood on the crest of the ravine below us. His head moved jerkily like a squirrel, while his torso remained motionless.

"Who is he? What's he doing?" I whispered.

Ronny stared. "Getting used to his new body, to being here again. I don't know him, but the big one has to be Cane. It's Erskine Cane."

The big man was as large as a house, and his head was nearly shaved. He was fairly busting out of his shirt. It hung nearly in shreds on his shoulders and arms, but I could tell that it was a camouflage shirt.

My heart shuddered. He was one of the soldiers who had given Abby Donner and her mother their seats on the train. Only now he looked terrifying. Mad. Crazy.

His face was angular and twisted into a bizarre smile. Even at that distance it scared me to my bones.

"I remember them both," I said. "They were soldiers on the train."

A siren stopped directly above us, and Ronny took my arm. His grip was cold, strong. He hustled me along the edge of the ravine, away from the stumbling policeman. Soon we were racing along a ledge in the hillside until the earth flattened out into a sort of meadow, its black grass scorched from the train fire.

"Come on," Ronny growled. "Come on."

So the farm boy who became a guard, died, and came back, pulled me along through the grass.

"Hurry," he said.

Scared, confused, angry, I followed.

FIFTEEN

Them

When we found a place that was out of sight, we poked our heads up and saw the two men scouring the bushes near the ledge.

What were they looking for?

I didn't want to think about it.

Cane gestured to the smaller man, and they moved up from the crest. The police still couldn't see them.

"I need to follow them," said Ronny.

"What? Follow them? We can't —"

"Who said 'we'?"

"You're not leaving me here!" I said.

But he was already scrambling away between brush and rock, heading deeper into the ravine. The police were hurrying down toward us. "Wait up!" I whispered.

Ronny — or Virgil, whatever — was amazingly sure-footed. After a few moments I couldn't see him anymore. I hurried to catch up but tripped over a rock, fell, and rolled twice, finally grasping at some roots to keep me from falling farther downhill.

The voices changed. They became garbled. My ear hurt, and I suddenly felt sick. Then I saw the wiry soldier creeping up behind Ronny. They knew we were there.

"Ronny!" I yelled. He didn't hear me. I tried the other name. "Virgil! Behind you!" It was too late. The smaller man grabbed Ronny from behind and held him still. Erskine Cane rose out of the bushes.

Cane towered over Ronny. His hands quivered at his sides, fingers flexing open, closed. He growled something, and Ronny spat something back at him. I was too far away to hear what they said. Were they arguing? I could make out a word, two. Then Ronny groaned as Cane pulled back and batted his face, while the other man held Ronny's arms tight behind his back.

I couldn't just stand there. "Stop it!" I yelled.

The savage head of Erskine Cane swiveled toward me. I went cold. Police cars were screeching to a stop on the ledge above. The officers on foot were still far behind us. Doors opened, slammed shut.

Cane had a military knife hanging on his belt, but he turned back to Ronny and relied on his giant fists, instead. Ronny's head was whipped back and forth by blow after blow, but he didn't make a sound.

Could he feel pain?

"Stop it!" I shouted again.

Cane was growling angrily with each breath. I crawled forward, then heard a rush of undergrowth crackling and crashing above me. Three officers hurried down the slope toward us, pistols out.

"Down on your knees, hands behind your heads!" one yelled.

Ronny fell limp to the ground as Cane and his sidekick bolted into the tall grass. Before they were out of view, Cane turned. His eyes flashed at me. I froze until the other man pulled him away.

One officer stumbled on the steep slope above, his pistol firing wildly. The others stopped. The cop was all right but, distracted, they were done chasing us for now. I pulled Ronny behind me, edging up the incline. He looked hurt, but there was no blood on his face. We raced toward the car, dived in. Ronny floored it again. This time, I was glad he drove with a lead foot.

He hunched over the wheel, silent, somber, eyes fixed on the highway ahead.

"What did he say to you?" I asked. "Cane. What did he say?"

No answer.

Maybe he knew I had heard his response to Cane. *You won't take him.*

"I heard something," I said. "Is he . . . are they after me? Are they after *me*?"

"I don't know," Ronny said softly. "Forget it for now. We need fuel. You have money?"

"Look —" I started.

"Forget it!" he said. "We need fuel!"

We drove into a small town, somewhere near Plauchville or Dupont. The town was nothing much — gas station, coffee shop, food mart, a handful of wooden houses, a trailer park. Three times as many cars were on blocks in the yards as on the street.

While Ronny gassed up the car, I went into the coffee shop.

It was the least dead thing I saw, and even it was empty except for one woman with her back to me, alone in a booth. Her hair was brown, stringy. She wore an ill-fitting denim jacket, a man's. She didn't look up when I entered, just went on drinking her coffee. She jerked it up to her mouth with both hands and bent to the cup halfway, as if she wanted to dive into it herself.

I didn't know why I looked at her for so long.

"Can I help you?" asked a smiling guy behind the counter. He couldn't have been much older than Ronny. Ronny could have had a simple job like that, taking orders, running the soda machine. Ronny could have done so much more than that. But not now. It made me sick.

I ordered a grilled cheese and a soda. The boy gave me a quick nod, swiveled to the soda machine, passed me my Coke, and disappeared into the kitchen.

I heard a spatula clank. The grill hissed.

I pulled out my cell phone. There were two missed calls and one voice mail from the same number — the New Orleans coroner. I listened to the message.

"Hello? Hello? Dang. This is John Runyon at the coroner's office? We have some information about . . . Carson Stone? From the accident?" Everything he said sounded like a question. "We got some bad news? Somebody call us back?"

He left the number and hung up.

The door squeaked. Ronny? I glanced up. No. A man came in and sat across from the stringy-haired woman, head low.

Next, the woman rose and crossed behind my back toward the restrooms. I thought for a minute that the boy in the kitchen had turned on the radio.

It wasn't the radio.

As the woman moved behind me, there was humming in my left ear. My cheeks flushed. My forehead got warm. It built and built as she approached, and died off as soon as she went by. It was a dull, low whisper by the time the ladies' room door closed behind her. I didn't get a good look at her. But I had heard words this time.

"*. . . first . . . first . . .*"

I shivered, colder than cold.

What did it mean? Was she one of them? Was she the crazy woman — Erskine Cane's wife?

Then it struck me who the woman — the body — might be. I almost fell off my stool. Abby Donner's mother? Had she died like the others and was now . . . translated?

It felt as if a needle were slowly being inserted into my neck behind my earlobe. I saw water, black water, as dark as the coffee in the counter pot. The woman emerged from the restroom. I turned to look at her, but her head was bent low. Her hair hung down, hiding her cheeks. She didn't look up, just walked slowly, mechanically, back to her seat.

The hum became a roar in my ears. "*. . . first . . .*" My blood went cold.

I paid, left, and hurried to the gas station. Ronny was sitting in the car.

"Anything?" he asked.

He said nothing when I told him what I had seen. I couldn't bring myself to understand what it meant if the woman I saw was actually the poor girl's mother. I was numb.

Three hours later, we were back in New Orleans. Ronny drove into the parking lot of the City Hall complex. I listened one last time to the coroner's voice mail.

"We got some bad news."

When we walked into the building, I wondered if I would know anymore what bad news really was.

SIXTEEN

The Dead Room

I was a wreck by the time we got down to the coroner's office, a gloomy set of rooms in the basement of the building behind City Hall. It was cold and smelled of chemicals.

Ronny, grim-faced, sullen, shuffled along behind me as if I were pulling him along.

The outer office was all oak chairs and benches. A secretary sat behind a wide desk. Beyond her, there were glass doors and streaky windows with the shades half pulled down.

"You here to see him?" she asked, without raising her head.

"Yes," I said. "It's about our father. Carson Stone."

"I know," she said, still not raising her head.

Saying his name, I saw Dad slide from the broken train. His cry was long, as if he were alive at least until the ridge at the top of the chasm.

Maybe the wreck didn't kill him.

Maybe he did survive.

Or was that blind hope? It had already been nearly a month.

The secretary pressed a button on her desk. A loud buzzer sounded, and a wooden door with reinforced glass clicked open on the other side of the little room.

"Go on in," she said.

Ronny followed a few steps after me, silent as a stone.

Inside was a room of shadows. Chilled and windowless, it had floor lamps at low wattage and one wall lined with refrigerated steel cabinets. I'd seen morgues on TV. I knew there were corpses in the drawers.

To one side, a huge man with spectacles at the end of his nose was leaning over a steel table, peering closely at something under an intense light.

Ronny stepped backward into the shadows.

"What are you doing?" I whispered.

"How much do I owe ya?" the man said then, without looking up from his table.

His white coat was open to show a wild printed shirt and cargo shorts. The armpits of the coat were dampened with sweat. I could see the floral pattern of his shirt right through them.

"Excuse me?" I said.

"Did you bring the po'boy?" the man asked, finally

glancing up at my empty hands. "I called back and asked for a roast pork with double cheese? Did you bring that, too?"

The look in my eyes must have told him.

"Wait. Pizza boy?"

I shook my head. "No. Someone called about our father."

Behind me, Ronny shifted his feet.

The man's face cleared. "You're *not* the pizza boy," he grunted. "So never mind." He toddled away from the steel table to a desk and rustled through a stack of papers. He slid one out.

"Your father is Carson Stone?" he asked.

"Yes, sir."

"Your mother around?"

"No. She's in France and isn't coming back."

"Then I got some news for you," he said, placing the paper back on the stack.

At that moment, the buzzer went off. The door clicked open again, and a girl walked in.

"Pizza," she said.

The coroner frowned at her, then laughed. "So *you're* the pizza boy!"

She didn't laugh. "Nineteen dollars, seventy-eight cents," she said.

"You bring the po'boy?" he asked.

"Porker, double cheese," she droned, sizing up his

barrel-waist. "And so good for you, too. That's nineteen dollars, seventy-eight cents."

He pulled out two tens and told her to keep the change.

"Gosh, what will I do with it all?" the pizza girl grumbled, slamming the door behind her.

In a single move, the man tore open the pizza box, detached a slice, and folded it deftly into his mouth.

"Your father's hand," he said, nodding me over to the table and prying open what looked like a plastic food container with his free fingers. Inside lay an assortment of pink things.

Blood rushed up my neck to my jaw, and my ear began to sting again. Did I hear voices? I turned, glanced at Ronny. He was immobile in the darkness, leaning against a file cabinet, eyes pinched shut.

"This here's a knuckle," the coroner said. With the bitten end of his pizza, he pointed to a knot of something at the bottom of the container. "I'm pretty sure of that. This other thing is part of a wrist. That little guy there might or might not be a finger. . . ." He went back to the steel table. "The DNA of these pieces says it's Carson Stone."

Hearing my father's name as I looked into the mess of stuff, my throat thickened up. "So what does this mean?" I croaked.

"Since they found these bits on the edge of the ravine," the coroner said, forcing the remainder of the slice into his mouth, "I'm pretty certain it means your father's dead. From there it's a sheer drop of near a hundred feet into a fast-moving river. If this is the only part of him they found, and they found it *there*, then you gotta conclude that the rest of him fell down the Gap into the river. It's like this, son. If the train wreck didn't kill him, if the rocks didn't kill him, if the long fall into the river didn't kill him, he surely would have drowned. You want my opinion?"

I wanted to say no, but my head nodded involuntarily.

"He didn't drown."

"You're saying my father's dead? He's definitely dead?"

Ripping a second slice out of the pizza box, he nodded. "I don't like to make things up, so I'll tell you. Yeah. He's dead."

There was a resounding knock, then the door swung wide a third time. A young woman entered, also in a white lab coat. "Fire in the Quarter," she said. "Police expect one, maybe more. They're saying arson."

My nerves jangled. *Arson?*

The coroner shook his head. "So supper'll have to wait."

He tapped his chubby fingers on the refrigerated cabinets, counting five over from the right side and three down, and jerked the drawer open. I expected to see a body inside. Instead, the drawer was filled with food and condiments. Two pickle jars, milk, yogurt, a bag of seedless grapes. He closed the lid of the pizza box and slid it and the sandwich into the drawer with the other food.

I took Ronny by the arm. He opened his eyes. He had the look of someone trying not to throw up.

We left through the door we had come in.

SEVENTEEN

The Running Begins

I tried hard not to think the worst — *arson!* — but by the time we got home, fire engines, police cruisers, ambulances, and television vans were everywhere. Streets had been cordoned off. The air was gray with falling ash and clouds of dark smoke. My heart iced when I saw the flames.

"Our house," I said. "Ronny! Our house!"

His face was dark. "Uncle Carl?" he said quietly. "Was he there?"

"What? No. He was away. He went away this morning. Our house! Oh, man —"

"Then who was the coroner lady talking about?" Ronny asked. "Did someone really die?"

I looked at him. "We can ask —"

"No," he said. "Don't let on that it's our house."

I couldn't do anything but watch the flames exploding out the front windows and reaching up toward the roof. The *faux chambre* was untouched so far, wrapped in thick scarves of smoke, but for how long? Flames spilled higher by the minute. Sirens shrieked close, then stopped. We pushed in as far as we could. Firefighters hosed the walls through the blasted windows. My eyes kept going back to the fake room. Why? What was there? Trains? Books?

"Do you hear them?" Ronny asked.

I listened. Over the sound of the roaring flames and water, I heard voices. "Yes."

"Cane did this," he went on. "You know he did. He found out where we live. He knows all about us. Wait here."

Ronny pushed through the crowd to a man wearing a tie and jacket, standing in the middle of a circle of cops. As he did, a shape moved up behind me in the darkness. I jumped.

"It's just me, Derek Stone."

I turned to see Big Bob Lemon, hunched over and staring up at the flames. He seemed smaller than the last time I'd seen him.

"Sorry about your home," he said in his low, rumbling voice.

I had to say it.

"You were there, weren't you?"

He turned his head, looked down at me.

"You were there in 1938, on that train that crashed into the Gap. You were nine, hiding out on that train. Weren't you?"

Lemon glanced over at Ronny, who was out of ear-shot. He nodded. "I was hiding out, yes. Boys did that then. I saw things happen that night. I dismissed them a long time ago, until your brother showed up and reminded me what I saw."

I knew it.

"You saw people die then, who are back now," I said.

Lemon nodded. "The dead are back. I knew it when that boy there came to me. He said things that proved he was the one who saved my life that day so long ago. He's that kind of boy."

I blinked. The ashes stung my eyes. "So Virgil was an okay guy? He's not like Cane at all?"

"Virgil Black was just a young man who happened to have a really bad first day of work. But the others who came back from that first crash? Murderers and arsonists. They found some way from their world to ours. A rift. And I'm talking rift with a capital R."

The Rift, I thought. The word took my breath away. It sounded horrific. But it explained it perfectly.

"Can it be closed?" I asked. "Can the Rift be closed?"

"Does a tear in a cloth ever become smaller?" he said darkly. "No, the road to the afterlife — it's a two-way street. How many dead have you seen so far?"

I thought about Cane and the other soldier. I believed that the woman at the coffee shop was Abby Donner's mother. The man who was with her was probably dead, too. "Five," I said. "Including Ronny."

"So far," Lemon added. "That leaves your daddy and three others we don't know about."

Ronny returned then, saw Bob Lemon, and nodded. "Somebody spotted a guy with a crew cut. They have some cars out looking for him. It was Cane."

"But what does he want?" I asked.

"To win," Ronny said.

"To win?" I said, glancing at Lemon. "What does that mean? Win what?"

"All of this. Here. The world. We're at war," Ronny said.

I looked into his face. "What?" I didn't — couldn't — understand.

"We're at war, the evil ones and us. We have been for ages. That's what's been eating at me since we went back to the Gap. There's a war, and it's been going on for centuries, and I'm a soldier in it. Only now, the war is spilling up here."

"But what about me? Why do they want me?" I asked.

"I don't know," he said. "I don't —"

Boooom! The second floor of my house burst into

flames now, and the police pushed the crowd farther back.

"I'm getting out of here now," Lemon said. "You should, too." His face was grim. He probably thought we wouldn't make it. Maybe he thought nobody would. Looking around nervously, he hustled off.

Ronny swung around on his heels. He tilted his head. "Cane!" he whispered. "He's still here. We have to bolt. Now!"

Ronny wrapped his cold hand around my arm and pulled. His grip was freezing. We ran down the sidewalks between houses, him pulling, me stumbling after. The voices surged again.

"They sense us near," Ronny said.

I looked back. Through the crowd I spotted the giant man and his wiry friend as if they were the only ones there. Cane's face was like the front of a truck. His arms were bowed as if his muscles were too big to allow them to hang properly. He was two hundred and fifty pounds of dead, running at us.

And there were three others with them this time, one of them a woman.

"Come on," said Ronny. *"Come on!"*

As we slid into an alley and flickered past the dark windows, the voices grew louder, wilder in my ear.

I ran as fast as my chunky legs would carry me.

EIGHTEEN

Public Transportation

"Where are we going?" I huffed. "We have no place to go!"

"In here," Ronny said when we reached the edge of the Quarter. We ducked into a narrow alley between two buildings. It was jammed with garbage cans. A large trash container loomed at the far end. The pavement was wet, blackly reflecting the facades on both sides.

I hurried on, cursing the fact that I was so overweight. Ronny let my arm go and shot ahead into the dark. He squeezed past the container and was gone.

I stopped. "Ronny?"

No sound now, except for sudden heavy breathing. It was my own chest sucking in, blowing out.

I ran to the trash container and leaned around it. No Ronny. Where had he gone? The lamppost above flashed on, then off, then flickered quickly, as if huge amounts of electricity were flooding through the wires. I couldn't see. Where had Ronny gone? My stubby fingers shook like dry leaves.

"Ronny!" I yelled.

The alley ahead was strangely quiet. All sound had been sucked out of the air except the faraway strain of a lone trumpet. It echoed from a few streets over.

My chest trembled hot and cold. I thought I would vomit. I walked down the alley, turned a corner. Decatur Street flashed neon blue, orange, blue, orange. I felt sicker by the minute.

Then Ronny was behind me. His grip on my arm was sudden, cold. "This way."

"Where were you?" I asked.

"This way," he said again. His face was iron, white, immobile, his eyes fixed on another cluster of trash cans at the far end of the alley. He walked toward them, then slowed.

"What is it?" I whispered, seeing nothing.

Ronny didn't speak.

I looked again. A shape rose slowly against the light, glowing blue, then orange, then blue again. It was the giant with the crew cut, a massive shape as dark as night, rising. In profile at first, his head turned to us. He grinned.

"Get out of here!" said Ronny, pushing me back.

But I couldn't. I couldn't. Three more shapes appeared and backed us against the trash cans. I tried to climb onto one of the cans, but it rolled, and I fell.

Out of nowhere, the wiry man leaped at Ronny, making a crazy noise in his throat. Two more shapes joined in. The one in the front was the train conductor, his uniform in tatters, his eyes sick and yellow. One sleeve dangled loosely. He had lost an arm in the wreck. It didn't slow him down.

Ronny fell to the street. The wiry man tumbled with him. Ronny leaped up and scuttled past the conductor. Cane watched with dead, black eyes.

I threw myself at the third attacker from behind. He was another passenger from the train, a gray-haired man. I didn't know what I was doing, but I moved as quickly as I could. The man tripped and went down. He growled a horrible noise, then tried to get to his feet, his head twisting up at me.

I surprised myself by stamping hard on his back. The man scraped his knees, shred his pants on the pavement, and fell flat again. He groaned, then laughed as if possessed. "Ha! Ha!" The sound was unearthly.

The woman was there now. Abby Donner's mother. She ran at us.

"Ladder!" Ronny yelled, pushing me toward a wall ladder glinting in the alley light. "Get up there!"

I struggled up the wet rungs to the rooftop, with Ronny an instant behind me. The roof was flat, bordered by a high wall in the rear. A rusty door stood in the wall.

"The roof!" came a screech from below. It was the one-armed conductor. The ladder rungs squealed as two, three sets of leather soles climbed up. Cane was not among them. *What is he waiting for?*

I yanked open the door. Ronny and I plunged inside the building. It was dark. He rummaged a pipe from a pile of scrap and slid it through the handle, past the inside of the door frame.

Almost instantly, we heard banging on the outside of the door.

"Hurry," Ronny said. We crept along a railed balcony on an inside wall overlooking an array of ugly machines, table saws, cartons, forklifts, sacks of grain or sand. We found a door, jerked it open onto a street opposite the alley, and raced out.

The woman and the gray-haired dead man were waiting for us.

"How —" I started.

Ronny faked a lunge at them, pushing me back through the door onto the floor and slamming it behind him. "Ronny!" I yelled.

The noises from outside were awful, inhuman, like animals at a kill. I heard a wild cry, then footsteps stuttering away into the night. I tore the door open. The alley was empty. They were all gone. So was Ronny.

I slumped to the ground, nearly sobbing. Ronny had drawn the dead away from me. But was he quick enough to get away from them?

The pavement gleamed in purple neon. I heard a police siren, two, three, in conflicting rhythm in the distance, all closing in. Had someone seen us fighting? Could the police help me?

There was a crash of glass, crystals sprinkling the ground, then the sound of heavy footsteps.

I spun around. A lone man walked toward me slowly, his sausage arms pumping like pistons. Erskine Cane.

This was what he had been waiting for.

I ran north into the streets around the park. I kept running. Cane's footsteps followed me relentlessly. The sirens were only a distant wail now, crisscrossing the sound of the dead. Was someone there? Anyone?

I was in a part of town I didn't know. A maze of dark streets. I should have stayed in the Quarter. Never mind. Cane was near, and I had nothing to fight with but my hands. Fat hands. Stubby fingers.

The voices in my head were deafening now. Growling. Shouting. Cane moved along the pavement toward me. I burst out of an alley and saw a streetcar rumbling along on its tracks. Yes! If it stopped, people might get off. I could mix with them, get lost in the crowd.

Maybe.

If it didn't stop, I might be able to run fast enough to climb on. Would it be crowded? Cane wouldn't do anything with people around. Would he?

I had to try.

My thick legs hustled toward the rolling car. The streetcar wasn't slowing. Cane hurried after me with loping steps, increasing strides. I kept running, pushing a teenage couple out of the way. They yelled after me. The car shuttled along more quickly than I expected. I wasn't going to make it. Cane was ten paces behind me. Eight. I faltered.

A white hand suddenly reached out from the crowded streetcar. It slapped onto my arm. I screamed like an idiot.

"Jump for it!" called a voice. "Derek – jump for it!"

I looked up. My heart nearly exploded.

I was looking into the face of my father.

NINETEEN

The Hand

He pulled me onto the streetcar with one hand.

"Dad!" I cried. People stared as I tumbled to the streetcar's floor. "Dad! Dad!" It was like I was struck dumb except for that one word. "Dad!" I wrapped my arms around him. "Dad —"

He stiffened and pushed me away. I saw his eyes — tired, hard — scan the receding street.

Cane was nowhere in sight.

My father was huddled and filthy. His beard looked a month old. His shirt was ripped and ill-fitting. The raincoat on his back was stained, shabby, and not his. These weren't the clothes he had worn on the train with Ronny and me.

"How did you — where were you —"

"Quiet!" he said, squeezing my arm like a vise. I tried to see both of his hands. The car was too crowded. I couldn't.

"Ronny is alive!" I blurted out, then hushed myself. "Ronny is here. Everyone thinks you're dead —"

More people looked.

"Shhh!" he hissed. "Listen —"

"But, Dad —"

"Listen to me!" he snapped. "I know about Ronny. We can't talk now. They're everywhere. More than you think —"

"More?"

Dad scanned the passengers quickly, squinting in the gray light of the streetcar's lamps.

I wouldn't let go of him. "I can't believe you're back —"

"There are dozens of them all over," he continued. "I have to hide. Look, I saw something happen in that ravine. The river, it . . . opened . . ."

I saw the water, too, felt it surround me — then shook it off. "I know," I said. "Ronny told me the same thing. Only he's not . . . he's not Ronny."

Dad's eyes searched my face for a second. "There's a way to close it. I think there is. It's . . . complicated. But before we can do anything, I have to go —"

"Go? No, Dad, you can't leave me again —"

He shook off my hand, raised his own hand to his forehead and massaged it, over and over. His eyes scanned the other streetcar passengers.

"There's no choice," he grunted, pulling me toward the rear of the car. "This is dangerous."

"Everything okay back there?" hollered the conductor, watching us in the rearview mirror.

"Oh, shut . . . yes! Fine," my father shouted. He was annoyed, angry. "Everything's fine." He drew me closer, shifting his gaze to the streets again. "Go to the cemetery. To the old tomb. The original one."

"The original . . ." I wasn't sure what he meant.

"The Longtemps tomb," he said.

"Mom's family? Why that one?"

"There's a message there," Dad snapped. "About where to meet me. I can't tell you more. Not here. We need to split up now."

I couldn't leave yet. I had to know.

"How did you survive the crash?" I asked.

The streetlights flickered blue, green, amber in his eyes as we passed the late-night music clubs. The car traveled slowly, but Dad's head was swiveling around like a crazed searchlight. It reminded me of what the short man did at the ravine.

"You didn't fall into the river, did you?" I pressed.

"I can't tell you now," he said. "I don't know. I don't remember that. The fall was . . . I don't know."

He was struggling with words. It was hard to watch his face contort. He was so different. Dad had changed so much from that day at TrainMania. His face twitched with fear. I tried again to see his hands, but he kept one buried in his raincoat pocket. Remembering the coroner's plastic container made my stomach roll over.

"The dead are walking again," Dad whispered. "They're coming together. It's horrible. But you — you saw something, Derek —"

"Me?"

"You saw something that night ten years ago in the bayou, and you need to remember it."

"Dad, no. What?"

He took my chin in his hand and stared into my eyes. "The girl," he said. "If she wakes up, you have to find her."

"What girl?" I said. "Dad, this is crazy. You mean Abby? The coma girl?"

"The girl from the train. If she wakes up, you have to get to her. Find her. Find . . ."

The car slowed. Some passengers climbed down onto the street, oblivious to the terror in their midst. At the same time, three people hopped into the front of the streetcar.

After the car started up, I shifted on my feet, trying to get a glimpse of them. My knees weakened.

My ears rang with voices.

One was the wiry man. Another was the woman from the alley, Abby Donner's mother. The third was a tall man with his head bowed. He turned to me. Cane. His lips curled into that mad smile.

My chest went ice cold. "Dad —"

"So, you can sense them," Dad said to me, following my gaze. "You can use that."

He stepped toward Cane.

"You can't fight him, Dad," I said. "He's a killer. He's got weapons —"

Trapped by traffic, the car lurched to a halt, and Cane rushed at us. My father swung me behind him and pushed. I nearly toppled an old woman.

The next seconds were a blur.

Something flashed in the dim light, sliding sharply down the silver hand pole. The sound of ripping cloth echoed in my bad ear.

"Ahh!" My father sucked in a huge breath.

A woman screamed. "He stabbed that man!" she cried, pointing at Cane. "He stabbed him!"

"Dad!" I cried. Cane's arm went low and started up toward Dad's chest. I kicked the giant's kneecap, and he fell back slightly.

"Get off me, you!" said an older man, pushing Cane from behind.

A shape hustled over from the far end of the car. I cowered. We couldn't fight off another one. We couldn't.

But it was Big Bob Lemon, his teeth set in anger. How he got there, I can't tell you. He hurled himself at Cane — the eighty-year-old guy did this! — knocking the dark hulk backward. Cane hit the floor of the car, taking three people down with him. Everyone was shouting, screaming.

The conductor set off an alarm. "I'm alerting the police!"

My father hung back, hunched over, still.

I thrust a man aside to get to Dad, but a strong hand took my shoulder from behind. Who did that? The conductor kept blowing his whistle, and I heard a police siren *whoop* through traffic nearby.

My father swung toward me. "Derek, you know something that will stop them. Keep it safe —"

"What?" I said. "What are you talking about?"

He struggled to say something — or *not* say something. "You were always smart, Derek. Be smart now —"

Cane was on his feet again. He reached out with one of his piston arms and ripped me away from my father. He dragged me to the front of the car and pushed the conductor into the street. The car jerked forward. Cane's fingers were like an iron vise, crushing my arm as he pulled my face to his. The hollow eyes, the black teeth — he reeked of death.

I screamed like a baby. It felt as if the bones in my shoulder would snap. I sank to my knees.

My father and Lemon ran forward, battering Cane's grip again and again until I was free. I tried to stand, but my knees buckled and my left foot slipped off the streetcar's deck. I grabbed wildly for the handrail, but missed.

"Dad —" I yelled.

"Go where I told you!" he shouted back at me.

I tumbled into the street as the car hurtled onward. Police converged on it.

I ran the other way, pushing through crowds, still feeling the giant's cold grip on my shoulder. I pushed through the midnight crowds until I found a deserted alley between two busy streets. I slumped to the ground, breathless and sick.

For minutes, I didn't move. My ears burned.

I tried to understand it all, then gave that up and began to cry. It was too much. It had to end. I wouldn't be able to take it.

But I had to take it. I had to.

My father was alive!

It gnawed at me that I hadn't seen his other hand. It sounds terrible, but I wanted to see blood. I wanted to know that, as banged-up as he was, Dad had somehow made it out of the ravine alive. That he wasn't like the others. That he wasn't like Ronny. His clothes were wrinkled, wet. His face was cut and scratched. He had a gash on his forehead. But it was night. The lights from the street, the shops, the restaurants, were garish. Was he bleeding? I couldn't tell. I couldn't tell!

I needed to find Ronny. Where was he?

Never mind that now. No. I had to go to the old tomb. The very thought made me shiver. The tomb was in the most ancient section of St. Louis Cemetery, in the oldest neighborhood of the City of the Dead, where not even workers dared go after the sun went down. That was where my father was sending me.

I had to go.

TWENTY

Run. Run.

The night air was close and wet as I approached the oldest part of the oldest boneyard. Its tombs stood silent, row upon row, like a derelict city, long abandoned by the living.

As I searched for a way over the wrought-iron fence, an old joke came back to me.

Why do cemeteries have fences around them?

Because people are dying to get in.

Only the opposite was true. People were dying to get *out*. According to Ronny, to my father, to Big Bob Lemon, to everyone, they were all dying to get out.

And they weren't coming to haunt us. They were a gathering army of the dead, and they wanted us dead, too.

Dead, or worse.

I thought I heard a sound. I turned, and saw headlights. Pickup trucks, two of them, circled the cemetery from different directions. I almost wished they were after me. Real people in real trucks. Not the dead.

My blood froze from my forehead on down. Dad said I know something? I saw something? What do I know? What did I see?

Never mind. I had to move. I found a loose gate and squeezed between it and its iron frame. I scratched my shoulder and knee, but didn't stop to look. My knee stung, and it felt good.

Once inside, I took a moment to get my bearings.

The old tomb, he'd said.

Not the tomb where the memorial was, but the Longtemps tomb. The tomb of my mother's family. What did *she* have to do with this? Why *her* family's tomb? She hadn't been around for ten years. She didn't even know that Ronny was . . .

Never mind. Focus. Find the tomb.

I wound through the narrow cemetery streets. I'd been to the old tomb only once before, a few days before my mother left.

I remembered it now.

It was a rainy morning, gray. The graveyard streets were puddled with black water. I told my mother I was afraid of water. But she took my arm and led me to the tomb. She talked. She said things.

What things?

She knelt to me, crying as she held my shoulders and kissed me.

Why? What did she say?

And suddenly the memories faded because I found it.

A tall, narrow house made of alabaster but blackened by grime, the Longtemps tomb shone yellow under a flickering streetlamp. On the curb in front of it lay a loose bunch of flowers.

My knees dampened through my pants when I knelt to the gravel. I heard a lone trumpet three or four cemetery streets over. It was late for a mourner.

Bah-dep! Dep!

A sudden footstep. I rose into a crouch, prepared to run.

"It's me," said Ronny, appearing beside me.

"Where have you been —"

"Who left the flowers?" he asked without emotion.

I read the card. One word: *Bonton*.

"Bonton?" said Ronny.

"It's Cajun slang for 'good times,'" I said. "You know that." No, I had to remind myself. *Ronny* knows that.

I felt like sobbing. Burning-hot air heaved up from my lungs. This wasn't going to stop, was it? The insanity was growing around me. It moved closer, took over every normal thing in my life. Up wasn't up anymore. Down wasn't down.

Dead Ronny. Maybe not-dead Dad. Big Bob Lemon. A piece of knuckle in a sandwich box. The false room. Daddy Jubal. Angola Freight. Erskine Cane. Virgil Black. Abby Donner, the coma girl!

Is this my life now?

"I remember him," said Ronny slowly. "There was a guy named Bonton. Bonton Fouks."

"When? In 1938? In Shongaloo?"

"Bonton Smitty Fouks," he said again. "No, he was a friend of your . . . of Dad's."

I stood up, blood rushing to my head. "You remember that? I mean, the Ronny stuff is still there? Are you . . . coming back?"

He growled. "Shut up. I don't know. It's a mess in here. All I know is there was a guy named Bonton Fouks who lived in a place called Bayou Malpierre."

Bayou Malpierre.

"Are you kidding me?" I said.

The nightmare rushed over me — I couldn't breathe, couldn't move, and the dogs were after me again.

I sucked in as big a breath of air as I could, but I couldn't fill my lungs. "I don't like bayous."

"Well, I don't like people cutting me up, either!" he

snapped. "Or hunting your poppa or burning your house or trying to take you —"

"Take me?"

"You can't be here alone."

"So where have you been for the last few hours?"

"Don't . . . don't ask me that," Ronny said. "Just don't. I don't know how to tell you what it is, or *where* it is, and you wouldn't want to know. But I'll help you."

I looked into his face, twisted in pain. "How?"

"I'll help you find your father . . . *our* father," he said with a kind of shrug. "I want to go back. I want to rest with my family again. On the other side. I don't like it here, but I . . . I can't leave you alone. Maybe I can remember things. Maybe I can protect you. I'll try."

Somehow, that made me more sad than glad. I needed him. But the fact that he *knew* I needed him, that I couldn't get on without him — a dead person I didn't really know! — made me feel like giving up.

"It's a clue," Ronny said, extending his hand. "We need to go to the bayou. Come on."

I looked toward the city beyond the fence. I saw the night oozing through its streets. I wanted to see the sun creep up out of the dark and illuminate the world, dry everything up. But the sun was so far away. It seemed farther away every second. I was living in the dark now.

A noise sounded, only it wasn't a trumpet this time. It was the squeal of a gate on the far side of the cemetery.

Then, with a sudden intake of breath as if the whole city paused to listen, there came the *thud, thud, thud* of shoes pounding and twisting the cemetery gravel.

Ronny's eyes were wild. "Them."

I saw the moving shapes in the distance. Five. Six. Seven.

I knew then what I hadn't been able to believe before. The dead really *were* after me. They wanted me. But why? *Why?*

Ronny nodded toward the fence. "We've got to go. Bayou Malpierre."

I took his hand. It was cold, a grip of death, but it was tight against my palm. He pulled. I followed.

With the sound of footsteps closing in behind us, we ducked between the tombs, hoisted ourselves over the fence, and made for the open streets.

We ran.

Bayou Dogs

To Those We See Again

CONTENTS

ONE

Speeding Up

The night streets slithered in front of us like dark snakes. They urged us every wrong way, crisscrossed one another, coiled back on themselves, stopped abruptly.

My brother Ronny wasn't having any of it. He kept running straight, feet slapping the wet pavement. His hand gripped mine, dragging me forward.

Like madmen fleeing their shadows, my mind told me, *or the shadows of others.*

Like so many times before, I had no time to wonder where those words came from. I just ran past houses, shops, restaurants, through crowded alleys — the whole noisy mess of the French Quarter at night.

My footsteps pounded the ground, jarred my bones. I tried to dodge the puddles as I ran. No luck. I barreled on and hoped I wouldn't fall on my face. I couldn't slow down. I couldn't rest. I couldn't stop.

"This way," Ronny said. "Hurry up!"

"I'm hurrying," I said, gasping for air.

"Not fast enough!" he snarled. "They're gaining on us."

I already knew that.

We'd been racing through the streets for over an hour in the middle of the night. We still couldn't shake them. No matter where we ran, the low voices pierced my ear, whispering, hissing, growling a mile behind us, half a mile, getting closer. Horrible voices.

Their voices.

They used to be people, but they weren't people anymore.

They were the dead. And now they were back.

The shadows of others, my mind said again. I shook my head. There were a lot of things I didn't understand rattling around up there.

"Behind us and to our left," Ronny said. "Five minutes at most. I hear them calling each other."

I nodded. "So do I —"

"Well, thanks to you, we can't outrun them," he snapped, throwing down my hand. "We have to hide. Follow me."

Ronny was angry, but he was right. I was out of shape. I did slow us down.

He turned abruptly and entered a side street. It was darker there. Two of the three streetlamps were out. The third flickered. Ronny scanned the houses on both sides of the street, looking for a vacant one. I watched his eyes dart back and forth, grateful for the chance to stop running. My lungs burned, my throat ached, my knees quaked under me.

I was fat. I was scared. Life was speeding up. Everything around me was spinning. I hated it. School, friends, family, home — everything I knew — was gone.

"Keep it down a little," Ronny said. "You're moaning again."

Maybe I was. You'd be moaning, too, if you were in my shoes. You might be, soon enough.

Ronny turned his head slowly from side to side, then twitched. He took a short step toward one dark house, paused, took another step.

"That one's empty," he whispered. "Come on . . ."

He loped down the narrow side yard and up a set of wooden steps. He forced open the back door with a quick thrust of his arm. There was a splintering crack.

Ronny grabbed the door to stifle the noise.

"In," he said.

Stale air, thick with the odor of mold, breathed out at me from the opening. It felt like the house was gasping its last.

"It stinks," I said.

"Cover your nose," he hissed. "Do you want them to find you?" Pushing me inside, he looked out at the street one last time and quickly shut the door behind us.

Ronny was right about the house being empty. It had the sullen, hollow feeling of abandonment. Even the furniture was gone. I collapsed breathless on the floor. The boards were soggy and rotten. Rain had poured in through a busted window and puddled on the floor. My pants soaked through when I sat down. I didn't bother to get up. I couldn't. I didn't care.

"Ronny —" I started.

"Quiet. They're less than a mile away. They'll hear you."

He was right about that, too.

The dead were coming. They were coming for me.

TWO

The Hard Way

My name is Derek Stone. I'm fourteen. And I'll try to make it as simple as possible for you to understand. The dead have come back.

Impossible, right?

Yeah, I wish. If you want the short version, it began a few weeks ago when a train carrying my brother, my father, and me crashed into a steep ravine called Bordelon Gap. Nine passengers were killed. I was lucky. I survived.

Ronny wasn't so lucky. He died.

Sort of.

It's complicated.

I'd found out the hard way about a thing called *translation*. My term. At the very moment of death, when a soul flees its dying body, another soul — one that's been dead for a long time — can take its place and reanimate that body.

How do I know? I know.

First, there are rules I've learned about translation. And no, I didn't make them up. That's something you need to know about me. I don't make things up. Ever.

To begin with, translation can only occur when both people died in identical ways. That's how it was with Ronny. A train had crashed at Bordelon Gap way back in 1938. It was a prison train, carrying a crew of nasty convicts. Because the convicts died just like the victims of my crash, some of them were able to translate into the bodies of the new victims. Ronny's body was taken over by a young prison guard named Virgil Black, who died in that first wreck. Strangely, some bits of my brother were left in him, glimpses of the brother I grew up with, which is why I still call him Ronny.

But with each day, there is less and less of Ronny . . . never mind that now. You'll see.

Back to business. Translation can only happen because of the *Rift* — not my term. I had dug around in old books, searched the Internet, scoured dusty archives, met a handful of strange people, and it all came down to this: The worlds of the living and the dead are separated by a thin, nearly impenetrable fabric. The living — people like you and me — stay on our side. The dead stay on their side.

At least they did.

Sometime in the recent past, the fabric separating the two worlds was ripped. The tear allowed dead souls to slip across and invade dying bodies. Virgil says they've wanted to do that for a long time. Bordelon Gap is — you guessed it — on the Rift.

You don't believe souls can come back from the dead?

Believe it. The road to the afterlife is a two-way street.

Finally, and this is the worst part, the dead are coming back because of the war.

The War.

Ronny jerked away from the window and walked from room to room, obviously searching for something. I was about to ask him what, when he came back with a beat-up broom in his hands.

"Going to clean up?" I asked.

Ronny snapped the long handle over his knee and tossed away the bristled half. Then he swung the three-foot, jagged-tipped stake in the air. "I'll clean up. If I'm lucky."

He scowled and took his position at the front window again. When he did things like this, I wasn't talking to my brother. I was talking to the country boy who had become a fighter in the War.

Virgil remembered bits and pieces about his seventy years in the land of the dead. He told me about a conflict between good and evil that has gone on for centuries. And guess what? Things weren't going so well for the good guys. They were completely outnumbered by dark souls who wanted to annihilate them.

The land of the dead?

I couldn't help imagining vast crumbling cities, teeming with souls twisted by their own evil. And then one day, a spark, a rebellion, a war. From that moment on, there was no going back. The evil fought the decent dead — souls like Virgil, who tried to stop them — and century upon century passed . . . until the fabric tore and the Rift opened. The dead saw their chance to reinhabit the world they left behind, to spread the War among the living.

So they came back.

One of dead who returned is a man named Erskine Cane. Remember that name. Erskine Cane was an arsonist on his way to be executed when the train carrying him and other convicts crashed at the exact place my train did. His twisted soul returned in the body of a young soldier with a crew cut and muscles from here to Houston.

Another convict entered the body of a second soldier, a short, wiry-limbed guy with a weird nervous tic. I called him Twitchy. The conductor from my train was back now, too, though he'd lost an arm in the crash. A gray-haired man I'd fought in the Quarter was another passenger from my train now inhabited by a dark soul. And Cane's mad wife, the only woman in the group, was also in a passenger's body. There were three others out there somewhere — I had seen only their shadows so far — all in bodies of the victims of my crash.

I know. I don't want to believe it, either.

"Why are they taking so long?" Ronny wondered aloud, moving from window to window.

I checked my watch. We'd been running and hiding for nearly two hours already, but as close as the dead sounded at times, they weren't on top of us. The voices closed in, coiled off, then came in again. It sounded like they were circling away and back like waves in a tide. It gave me time to think about how lucky I am.

No, really.

I'm lucky. Virgil Black is one of the good guys. Before he died in the first wreck, besides being a farm-fresh country kid, he had saved the life of a little boy. That boy grew up to be Bob Lemon, now an old musician who had joined our fight against the dead.

All Virgil Black really wanted was to be dead and at peace — but there was no peace, here or there since the War escalated, and he didn't know how to get back there anyway. So he stayed.

I like to think that he stayed to help me. Although right now he was being a snot about my weight.

"Hey, Chubs, how far is Bayou Malpierre?"

Oh, right. There's that, too.

"Five, six hours," I told him. "That bayou's hard to get to."

"Of course," Ronny said. "Everything else is hard. Why not that?"

As if I wasn't dealing with enough weirdness already, Bayou Malpierre was where I nearly drowned when I was four years old.

We had to go there now because — get this — my dad, who everyone believed had died in the train crash, suddenly showed up and told me and Ronny to go to Malpierre and wait for him.

What? After everything else, you think *that's* weird?

Ten years ago, Bayou Malpierre had been all darkness and rain. I was lost in the swamps. I was afraid. Dogs were coming. And I fell into the water. I tried to claw my way to the surface. Water poured into my nose, my ears. My lungs wanted to burst open —

"You're moaning again," said Ronny, his eyes flashing at me now.

"Sorry," I said.

"Just keep it down."

No one knew who had saved my life that night. Not my father, not Ronny, not my mother — I hadn't seen her for the ten years since the bayou incident, anyway. But being in the water so long had damaged my left ear — the ear that could now hear the voices of the dead.

Told you it was complicated.

Ronny parted the curtains carefully and looked out. I did, too. The only streetlamp with a glimmer of life shone dull brown and then sick yellow on the glazed pavement.

Guttering like a failing candle flame, I told myself.

I was really getting annoyed with these random words that kept popping into my mind. I shook my head and focused on the street. Nothing. Not yet.

"Do you think we should move on?" I whispered.

"To where? To your house?" Ronny said. "Think about it."

I felt like saying, "You start," but kept my mouth shut. Since he died, Ronny had no sense of humor.

But he was right about my house. Erskine Cane had torched it just hours before. Why, I'm not sure. But Cane was after me. I knew that.

"Ronny," I started, "about Cane —"

All of a sudden, my cell phone rang.

"Turn that thing off!" Ronny snapped.

"Sorry," I said.

I opened the phone and noticed that I had only two battery bars left. It was Uncle Carl calling. He had been living with us since the crash. He'd been in Oregon on a business trip when our house burned down, but he'd now just now heard about the fire. He was crazy with worry.

"The alarm company finally tracked me down!" Carl yelled in my ear. "There was a break-in at the house? Then a fire? Are you boys okay? What's going on?"

A break-in? I didn't know that part. I lied and told Carl that we were spending the night at my friend Tooley's house. Ronny and I would be meeting with the fire marshal in the morning. I lied and lied. I didn't know exactly what we were doing, but I knew we couldn't stay put. Carl was smart, but easy to fool. He trusted me. I felt like a criminal.

Right. Me, a criminal. Chubby boy, Derek Stone. Me, running for my life from dead people. *I'm* the criminal!

"So you're both all right?" Carl asked, clearly relieved. I told him we were. "I'm coming right home, anyway," he said. "I'll be back there later today."

"We'll see you tonight at Tooley's house," I lied. I had no idea where we'd be tonight. If we'd be anywhere at all.

Carl said he would let the police know that we

were fine. We hung up, and I tucked my phone in my pocket.

"Try to keep that off until we need it," said Ronny, stalking quietly from window to window as if he'd done this sort of thing before. Watching him reminded me of his fight with Cane at Bordelon Gap. I thought of Cane's equally twisted wife again. From what I knew, she was now in the body of the mother of a girl who had been on the train with us.

A girl who was in a coma.

A girl named Abby Donner.

She was the most recent piece of the puzzle.

Dad told me to wait for him in Bayou Malpierre, but he also said I had to talk to Abby Donner if she ever came out of her coma. Why? I don't know.

I don't know much, really.

Ronny tensed at the window.

I went to him. "What is it?" I whispered.

Peering between a pair of filthy curtains, I spied a shadow moving in and out of the light. It was a figure, tall and thick. "Oh, no, no, no . . ."

"Quiet," Ronny said.

"Can you see his face? Is it —"

"Quiet!" he snapped.

The figure moved out of view. I cocked my bad ear. Why were the voices so quiet? I turned my head. Where were they?

For minutes, we didn't move.

Then there was a click at the back door.

I heard the door swing open and tap against the inside wall of the kitchen. I couldn't breathe. My lungs burned. My heart hammered. I looked for a weapon, picked up the other half of Ronny's broom, and held it out like a bayonet.

Footsteps sounded heavily on the floorboards. Ronny crept behind the door, his pointed broom handle aimed high.

Thunk . . . thunk . . .

The door flew open.

THREE

Casualties of War

"Derek Stone . . ." A low voice rang through the darkness.

A shape teetered in the doorway, then fell forward, a dead weight at my feet.

"It's Bob Lemon!" I cried, rushing to him.

"Shhh!" said Ronny, at my side. He bent down and tilted the old man's head forward. A great breath came from his mouth.

"They're near —" Lemon whispered.

"What happened to you?" I asked. Only hours ago, Lemon had helped my father battle Cane on a streetcar so I could escape. "What did they do to you?"

"Hamburgers did this to me!" he gasped, clutching the front of his shirt. His heart. "But never mind that. The girl . . . the girl is awake. . . ." He began to cough.

"What do you mean?"

"The girl!" Lemon grunted. "Something happened at University Hospital. I heard it on the news."

It hit me. "You mean Abby Donner? The girl in the coma?"

"Your father told me about her. It was just on the radio. Something happened. She bolted out of her coma like magic. She's awake —" He grabbed his neck.

"You need a hospital," I said, pulling out my cell phone.

"Put that away!" Lemon said, slapping the phone closed. "Find that girl fast. If your father told you to, there's a reason."

He went silent. Ronny propped up Lemon's head with some old kitchen towels he'd found. The murmuring in my bad ear was growing louder, closer. When I pressed my ear to try to stifle the pain, I made out five voices moving toward us. Closing in.

"We only have a few minutes," said Ronny, sneaking toward the windows in the back of the house. "No more than that. Bob, we need to move you."

"He's right," I added. "You can't stay here. I'll call —"

"No!" Lemon said forcefully. "Wait until you're out of here. And don't use your cell. You can't have the police tracing the call and connecting this with the house fire. They'll pick you up. You have to stay free. Use a pay phone. There's a hotel three blocks down with one. You need as much of a head start as you can get."

He was right, we had to keep moving. But it still hurt to see him in pain. I had only known Big Bob Lemon for a couple of days. Hours, even. Yet here he was, risking his life for me, for the second time in one night.

"Your daddy tells you to do something, you do it," he added.

"Yes, sir," I said quietly.

I could tell from his eyes that he was doing everything he could not to pass out.

Ronny squeezed Lemon's shoulder. "Derek, we have to go. Now."

"That's right, go!" said Lemon. "Stay alive, Derek. You have to stay alive —"

Stay alive. It sounded like an order. A command.

Ronny yanked me onto the back steps. He scanned the dark. "Now!" he whispered. We ran from yard to yard out of the light, all the way to the corner. I didn't look back.

It was nearly three in the morning and the streets were empty when we reached the hotel. "I'll stay out here to watch and listen," said Ronny. "Hurry it up."

I pushed through the revolving doors and saw a bank of phones near the elevators. I went to them, digging in my pockets for change. I had none, but there was a sticker on the phone saying that emergency calls were free.

I dialed 911, and a woman answered. She said something, but I spoke over her. "Border Street. Number 13. A man is having a heart attack."

"Your name, please?" she asked.

"Number 13, Border Street," I repeated as clearly as I could. "And use your siren." I hung up.

Then I was back on the street with Ronny, where the dark swallowed us up again. We ran away from the voices. Why I heard them, or why I'd been hearing them for days, I can't tell you, but I heard them. They hissed, squealed, shrieked, converging on the house loud and wild.

"Ronny —" I started.

"I know," he said, tugging me firmly forward. "If we could go back to him, I would. We can't. We have to keep moving. Get to the hospital, find the girl, get to the bayou. So run. Now!"

Told you life was speeding up.

FOUR

Room 754

It didn't take us long to get to University Hospital, but we had to keep out of sight until morning. Places like that pay special attention to anyone who tries to enter in the middle of the night without an emergency. Can't say I blame them.

Finally, eight AM came around, gray and hot and wet. By the time Ronny and I stepped up to the emergency room doors, I was a ball of sweat. I pulled my shirt away from my skin and wafted air into it.

Ronny gave me a look. "Pretty gross," he said.

Times like these convinced me that Ronny wasn't completely gone. There were still traces of my brother in this person. Could he possibly come back?

"Wanna sniff?" I asked, grinning.

But Ronny wasn't with me anymore. His face had turned to stone. It was already over.

"Follow me," he said, pushing his way through the double doors like a robot.

I followed him into the ER. It was buzzing.

Along with everything else — the blaring intercoms and droning chatter from the waiting room and behind the admissions desk — there was some big deal going on. From what I could tell, it involved an older woman and a couple of nasty-looking guys, all on stretchers and all yelling at one another. I silently thanked them. Their disturbance was a good cover.

Ronny and I slipped through the ER lobby and into the main building. As we searched for the front desk, I wondered what I was actually doing there. What did I expect? Could I even begin to explain to this girl what I thought — what I knew — was happening?

Was I going to tell her about her mother? "Excuse me, miss, your mom died, but not really. She's kind of a zombie, totally dead, way crazy, and a killer."

Right. That would go over well.

"Big place," Ronny said, looking around. "We need the girl's room number."

"We could ask," I said.

Ronny eyed the front desk. A group of men and women with cameras and microphones stood in a bunch with two security officers. "Reporters," he said. "If we didn't get turned away, we'd be put with them."

That impressed me. He had sized up the scene quickly. "Maybe we could sneak a look at the computer behind the main desk. I think the patients' room numbers are on the computer screen."

Ronny scanned the desk, thinking. "Okay, but we need a distraction."

"Maybe do something dumb?" I suggested. "If you can distract someone, I can try to get the room number."

"Dumb? Like what?" he asked.

"Like, I don't know, dumb," I whispered.

Ronny's face changed slightly as if he had formed a plan.

He swiveled on his heels, then pulled me around a corner. I had no clue what he was doing until he found a supply closet, slipped in, and came out a minute later wearing a blue work shirt. He tucked some white garbage bags in his belt. He handed me a similar shirt.

"What are we, janitors?" I asked, pulling the shirt on. "Couldn't you find some extra scrubs? I always wanted to be a surgeon —"

My heart quickened. A surgeon?

I took up the silver blade. . . .

Stupid words from nowhere again.

When I snapped out of it, Ronny was already heading toward the front counter in the main lobby. He nodded to me and stepped right up to the desk. Grinning, he made a big thing of unflapping a garbage bag.

"For the trash run this afternoon, miss," he said to the woman standing behind the desk, charming her like a true country boy. The woman smiled and pulled her chair back.

"Here you go," she said.

But as Ronny reached for her wastebasket, he fumbled and dropped it. "Oh, miss, I'm sorry!"

It actually looked natural. The contents of the basket — papers and tissues — spilled on the floor under her desk.

"Oh, dear," the woman said, stooping to help him clean it up. While she was facing away, I leaned over and scanned the patient list on her computer. "Donner, Abby" was near the bottom of the alphabetical list on that screen. Our little reconnaissance mission was a success.

I stepped away from the desk as Ronny gathered the last of the trash. He grinned at the woman. "I'm real sorry, miss," he said.

"It's ma'am," she replied, smiling. "And it's no problem."

"You have a good day," Ronny said, handing me the garbage bag as we walked away.

"Room seven-five-four," I said. "That was pretty good, by the way."

He shrugged. "I guess I can be sneaky."

We wormed back through the halls together and found an elevator. I tossed the garbage bag in a nearby can before we got in.

When the elevator doors opened on the seventh floor, room 754 was to our left. I could hear the bubbling noise of televisions up and down the hall. I began to imagine the room, and the bed, and then her.

A new thought hit me.

What injuries had Abby Donner suffered in the accident? I had seen her being thrown all around the crashing train car with my own eyes. She could be completely busted up. Did she still have all her limbs? Was she scarred? Blind? Crazy over her mother's death? What?

Just then, Ronny stopped. His shoulders tensed. He tilted his head.

"What's the matter?" I asked.

"I'll be back in a minute. Find her." He moved down the corridor, turned the corner, and darted out of sight. The sounds of the hospital buzzed in my ears, but I didn't hear any voices. Did he?

I took a deep breath and suddenly felt completely empty. I imagined the face of the Coma Girl. I didn't want to do this. I didn't want to see her.

But my father had told me to, and my feet took me forward. I found room 754.

Remembering the horror of the train wreck, I raised my hand and knocked on the half-closed door.

FIVE

The Donner Girl

"Who is it? Grammy? Come in. I'm ready to go."

Her voice was bright. Not a dead voice. Not damaged.

My nerves were electric. I pushed on the door and stepped in.

She looked like I remembered her. Her face hadn't been damaged in the crash, though it was pale. Being in a coma for weeks would probably do that to a person. She was dressed in normal clothes — shorts, T-shirt — and sat cross-legged on the bed with a book in her lap. She looked surprised for a minute when I came in. Then she nodded to the corner.

"Sorry, I thought it might be my grandmother," she said. "The wastebasket's over there. It doesn't have much in it because I've been eating through a tube, but last night's pudding cup is in there, from my first meal after I woke up. I was really hungry, but my stomach couldn't handle it. Don't worry, I made it to the bathroom to throw up, but I tossed the rest of it out —"

"Abby Donner?" I said, pulling off the janitor's shirt like a superhero, though I felt exactly the opposite. "Do you remember me?"

She frowned. "Remember you? Well, I don't know about me and memory. . . ."

While Abby searched my face, I noticed that her arms were scratched up, and — I hadn't seen it before — her foot was in a cast.

All at once, her eyebrows shot up. "The boy from the train! You made it! You survived —" She closed her eyes quickly. When she opened them again, they were wet.

I felt my cheeks get red. "I'm sorry about your mother," I said.

"I . . ." She nodded a few times, stopped, swallowed, and wiped her eyes. "They already had a service. There wasn't any . . . they haven't found her yet."

Which I knew, of course. Her mother's body was still walking around out there.

Abby said nothing else right away. Looking into her eyes made me uncomfortable, so I glanced out the window. The city outside was quivering with heat; the river was brown and slow.

"Anyway," she said, trying to lighten things up, "I

popped out of my coma yesterday. A miracle, they say. They've been monitoring me for weeks, and I'm pretty much healed after the accident, so they're letting me out today. I have to check in every three days, but otherwise, I'm good. My grandmother's coming to bring me home."

I smiled. "That's good. Really good. My name is Derek, by the way, in case you don't remember."

"Right," Abby said. "Thanks for coming." Her forehead wrinkled. "But why did you come? I mean, I know we were in the same crash together, but it's not like we really know each other. We don't, do we? I'm a little fuzzy from my coma. . . ."

I breathed out. There was no choice — I started.

"Okay. So, listen. You're totally not going to believe any of this, but I have to tell you some really strange stuff that's been happening since the train wreck. Impossible stuff. I don't even believe it myself, except that I don't really have a choice —"

"Nice buildup," Abby said, laughing nervously. "Do you even *want* me to believe you?"

"Well . . . yeah . . ."

Her smile flickered and died. *Like a failing candle flame,* I thought. Stupid words.

"Okay then," she said softly. "Tell me."

Before I could say another word, Ronny dashed into the room, still in his janitor's shirt.

"Hey, a reunion of survivors! What, no shirt for me?" Abby said, grinning.

"Sure, sure." Ronny tried to smile at her, then pulled me aside. "Look, I don't hear any voices yet, but I still don't like it. You'd better make it quick. We can't be anywhere too long. I'll scout for exits." He was gone as quickly as he had come in, a soldier on a mission.

"Aside from his pasty complexion and bad hair," Abby said after he'd gone, "what's his problem exactly?"

Some lead-in. I took it.

"That's sort of what I wanted to talk to you about," I said slowly. "Since the crash, I've seen some of the people who died in it."

"You went to their funerals?"

"Uh, no," I said. "I mean, the people are still around."

"You mean, the survivors —"

"No," I said. "They died, all right. Only . . . they're back."

Abby narrowed her eyes at me. "They're back?"

"Yes."

"They died, but they're back."

"Right," I said.

She nodded. "And I thought *I* was crazy from my coma."

"Look, no," I said. "At least you're not dead. And neither am I. But . . . my brother Ronny is. Ronny died in the crash."

"But I just saw him."

I took a breath. "Now you get it."

Abby's face fell. Her silence gave me a chance to try to put everything into some kind of order.

I told her how Ronny died and showed up one day, changed; how I learned that an earlier train had crashed in 1938; how I came to know that the souls from the earlier crash had entered the bodies of several people in our crash; and finally how I discovered that Ronny was now inhabited by the soul of someone named Virgil Black.

I also told Abby the bad news — wasn't it all bad news? — that most of the souls were dangerous convicts, and that they were after me for some reason I couldn't explain.

Her mouth hung open through most of this. She finally closed it and spoke quietly. "Dead people are after you?"

"I don't know why," I said, looking down at the floor. "My father told me I know something, but it's hidden in my memory or something. Anyway, he also told me I had to find you if you woke up."

"Me? Why me?"

I shrugged. "I was kind of hoping you'd tell me.

Maybe it has something to do with you being in a coma?"

"Uh-huh. Maybe," she said. "But I'm not going back into it just for you."

I smiled a little, then took a deep breath. "You don't hear voices, do you?"

She spun around, slid off the bed, hobbled to the window, and looked out — all without saying anything. Then she turned to me again. Her face was red. "Voices? Of course not! You're nuts, is what you are. Dead people coming back? It doesn't happen that way. They're dead. *She's* dead. Everyone knows that. My mother died in the wreck and that's all there is to it. She died and she's dead and she can't talk to me!"

I stared at Abby, not quite knowing how to react to this outburst. All at once, the anger fell from her face. She covered it with her hands and started to sob.

"It can't be true!" she said. "It's not possible. She isn't . . ."

A shiver of fear entered my chest. "Abby, did you hear someone?"

"No, no, no . . ." She sniffled loudly. "She's dead!"

"Your mother?" I said quietly. "Have you heard her?"

Her eyes flashed at me. Then, slowly, she nodded.

Climbing back on the bed, she said, "Just so you know, I don't go for make-believe, I don't. My whole life, I never had imaginary friends. I never even hung out with kids who had imaginary friends. I never played with dolls. I like sure things, like numbers, history. You can depend on all that —"

Huh. That sounded familiar.

"Abby," I said. "Did you hear your mother's voice?"

She raised her red eyes. "I think she came to see me."

I tried not to react. "She —"

"She came to see me when I was in my coma. She talked to me. Told me things. I *heard* her when I was — wherever you are when you're in a coma. Grammy said the nurses even told her they saw someone here, a woman, but she disappeared before they could talk to her. I think it was my mother."

"What did she say?" I asked.

Abby shook her head sharply. "But I can't have heard her, right? Because she died in the crash. She couldn't have —" She stopped, her face stricken with sudden horror. "My mother's not . . . she isn't one of the . . . you haven't seen her?"

"No!" I lied. "No. No. Nothing like that." I didn't know what else to say. I wasn't ready to talk about that. She wasn't ready to hear it.

Abby slumped onto her bed again, eyes filling with tears. "I guess I must have imagined it, right?"

"Tell me what she told you," I said. "In your coma."

Crossing her legs as before, with her ankle cast in her hands, Abby grew very quiet, very still. "She told me about a place. It was dark all around. No. Not all around. There was a big flash of light above her. And she said everything was wet. Like they were standing in a dirty lake or something."

Ronny had told me the same thing: It was wet.

"Where was all this supposed to be?" I asked.

She shook her head. "I don't know. There were people around her. Lots of them."

Lots. The word sounded sickening. "Do you mean 'lots' like, 'Wow, this cereal has *lots* of raisins,' or like, 'Wow, there are *lots* of people in the world'?"

Abby thought about it, then took a breath. "Like there are lots of people in the world, only . . ." She paused. "Only more. They all wanted to go through the flash of light. But only a few made it."

The Rift, I thought. My heart dropped to my feet. I felt dizzy, trying to understand. "Were you and your mother . . . close?" I asked.

Abby frowned. "Of course we were close. She was all I had. Aren't you and your brother close?"

I said nothing.

"So what do you think it means?" she asked.

I paced to the window and back. "I don't know how you heard what you heard. But I think — I think it means that the dead are gathering and waiting for a chance to return."

"Return?" Abby's face turned even more pale. "The dead are waiting to return? What for?"

All I could think of was the War. I was trying to work up to telling her about it, but Ronny burst into the room.

"He's here," Ronny hissed urgently. "Cane. We need to go!" He turned and disappeared through the door again.

I heard a growl echoing in my ear. I turned to Abby. "We're leaving. And you're coming with us."

"Me?" she snorted. "I'm waiting for my grandma —"

More voices. "Sorry," I told her. "We can't wait for your grandmother."

Abby burst out laughing. "Are you serious? *Everybody* waits for my grandmother! I was at a wedding once, and the priest was at the altar, ready to do the vows. Everybody, and I mean *every*body, in the church was waiting and waiting —"

"Tell me while we run!" I snapped.

I grabbed her arm and charged out the door after Ronny.

SIX

Express Checkout

The hall was jammed with gurneys, doctors, patients. Ronny tore through them and bolted around the corner. I hustled Abby along after him as quickly as I could.

"No running!" yelled a nurse.

Among the tangle of voices in my ear, I heard Cane's terrifying murmurs. The others, too — hissing, grunting somewhere in the halls. They were here and closing in.

"How did they find us?" I called to Ronny.

He was already far down the corridor, flashing through a set of doors that swung closed behind him. He kept running.

"Come on!" I said, turning back to Abby.

"I have a broken foot, you know —"

For once, someone else was slower than me. We clomped down the hall. Abby slapped her hand on the electric opener, the doors whooshed back, and we barreled through.

I raced around the first corner to my left, slammed into a nurse, and knocked a lunch cooler out of her hand. She screamed.

"Sorry!" I said, as the cooler tipped over and opened. I bent over to pick up what I thought was going to be her sandwich.

It wasn't a sandwich. It was a lung.

My stomach heaved into my throat.

Abby grabbed my arm and yanked me into a stairwell. "That was classic!" she said, laughing.

"I just knocked over someone's transplant!" I cried.

"They'll probably just wash it off —" she started, when I clapped my hand over her mouth.

The short soldier — the one I called Twitchy — stormed down the hallway past the stair door, his head twitching like a squirrel's. The conductor was with him. His empty, ragged sleeve dangled at his side.

"Holy crow!" Abby whispered, pulling my fingers away. "Is that them? They look so —"

"Dead?" I whispered. "That's them."

People yelled down the hallway, telling the two dead men to stop. But they just walked on.

I thought we might be in the clear, until Cane moved past the doorway. His crazy smile looked like a crescent moon, half-cocked up the side of his face. I hoped Abby's mother wouldn't show herself. Not yet. Please. Not now –

A high-pitched squeal rang through the hallway. It pierced my bad ear. A hand thumped my shoulder, and I nearly jumped out of my skin.

It was Ronny. He pulled me and Abby down the stairs behind him. "Come on!"

"Ow, ow, ow," she said. "My foot–"

At the next landing, Ronny ran through the door and quickly found a service elevator on the sixth floor. We all piled in. The doors closed behind us.

Before the elevator moved, there was a sudden kick on the doors. Ronny backed up, his finger to his lips. We heard a garbled noise out in the hall, but the doors didn't reopen.

A low voice outside the elevator.

Not Abby's mother.

Ronny tilted his head as the elevator moved away from the sixth floor. "That's a new one. Someone else from the crash," he whispered.

"How do you know?" Abby asked.

Ronny didn't answer before the elevator lurched and slowed. The doors opened on the second floor, and we barreled past a couple of doctors in green scrubs before they had time to stop us. Ronny stormed down the hall as if he knew exactly where he was going. It was strange to watch him. Was it coming back to him now, everything he had learned as a fighter in the war down there?

We approached an open staircase, which led down to the main lobby.

"Grammy might be out front by now," said Abby, hobbling along like a champ.

"Except we can't go that way," said Ronny, suddenly yanking my arm nearly out of its socket. "Out the back."

We turned and raced down the hall to the rear of the building. We leaped down the stairs there as quickly as we could with Abby's ankle in a cast. At the bottom stood a door with a red bar across it.

Ronny didn't hesitate. He grabbed the bar with both hands and pushed. The alarm screamed in our ears as we dashed out to the parking lot.

Abby looked around frantically. "There!" she cried, pointing. "My grandmother!" She pushed me at a minivan driving slowly along the side of the hospital, toward the pick-up circle up front. "Grammy!"

The woman at the wheel slowed, spotted Abby, and waved.

"I made hospital friends!" Abby said, staggering over to the car with me and Ronny. She tugged open the side door and pushed us into the backseat, then hopped into the front, pulling her foot in behind her. "Guys, meet Grammy Nora. Now, hit it, Grammy!" yelled Abby. "To the floor!"

"But, dear —" the woman started. All it took was a glimpse of the four mangy figures charging out the door after us, and she slammed her foot on the gas. The car burned rubber all the way into traffic.

SEVEN

On the Streets of Metairie

If Abby's grandmother had a heavy foot on the gas, it wasn't any lighter on the brake.

No matter how quickly we screeched down the street, Grammy Nora made a complete stop at every red light and stop sign. It was like the pulse setting on a blender. We were hurled back and forth in our seats until we felt sick.

"Good thing I didn't eat that pudding," said Abby, under her breath.

"You boys," said Grammy Nora, scowling into her rearview mirror. "I don't think I like whatever it is that you're mixed up in."

Abby turned to look at me and Ronny. "I think it's just a little misunderstanding. Right, guys?"

"Absolutely," I said.

Grammy Nora didn't seem sold.

After zigzagging from one street to another, Ronny asked Grammy Nora to head for the alley behind Royal Street. We needed his car. The minivan turned onto an avenue that ran straight toward the French Quarter.

Finally, the voices faded from my ear.

The silence gave me a minute to think. I realized that the dead had managed to find us everywhere we'd gone since yesterday — the Quarter, the cemetery, the abandoned house last night, the hospital this morning.

I didn't like it.

If the dead really were following me, they were finding me.

I knew I needed lots of time to think this through, but I wasn't going to get it. We had just turned off the avenue and roared into a mess of short streets when Abby jumped.

"Stop!" she screamed. "Grammy, stop!"

"What?" Grammy Nora said, alarmed. "But Abby, this isn't anywhere —"

Abby pointed to a large house that sat on a hill behind a big black fence. "There!"

Abby pulled on the door handle before her grandmother even slammed on the brake. She swung herself out of the car, nearly tripped over the curb, hopped up to the iron fence, and strained against it.

I followed her.

Over a rise of lawn behind the fence stood one of the grander houses in the Quarter, a three-story brick mansion. It had a broad, peaked front and tall white columns, which ran up from a porch that stretched across the front and sides of the house. The bricks were painted dark pink, but they looked gray in the hazy light.

I glanced back at Grammy Nora. She shrugged. Ronny looked anxiously at me from the backseat of the van.

"Abby, do you know this place?" I asked.

For a long time she studied the house and said nothing. Then she shook her head slowly and backed away from the fence. "No. Not this house. But there's something about it. The columns?"

A brown shade rippled in an upstairs window. Someone looked down at us. Abby turned away.

"I don't know," she said, narrowing her eyes in concentration. "Something about a house, not this one, but *like* this one. Derek . . ." Abby turned to me. "Did she really come to me in the hospital? My mother?"

I almost shrugged, but then stopped myself. "I don't —"

"She's one of those people, isn't she? One of the dead ones. You can tell me. Please tell me."

I saw her mother's image in my mind. Gray-faced, soaked, her hair matted, her eyes as black as onyx marbles. She had a horrible, stuttering, maniacal walk, and a gargling voice. I only understood one thing she'd said to me.

Firsssssst . . . firssssst . . .

"Never mind," Abby said quietly, shaking her head. "I believe it anyway. The dead are gathering. I think I get that. And there's something about a house. And about you. They're after you."

"I don't know why," I said for the second time in an hour. It was almost a whisper.

"But your dad thinks I can help you," she added. "Because of what I know. But how?"

"Maybe it's because of your mother," I said. "Maybe *she* knows something, and maybe she told you."

"How does your dad know about my mom?" Abby asked.

It was a question I hadn't asked myself before.

Abby took my arm suddenly, and I jumped.

"I remember something else she told me!" she said. "It was garbled. I couldn't make out most of it. But there was one word I understood. I remember it now."

She stopped.

I glanced back at the van. Ronny's eyes were riveted on Abby. He opened the car door and walked over to us.

"What word?" he asked. "What word was it?"

She was shaking. "Legion."

My veins turned to ice.

"I know the word," said Ronny, staring off into the east, where the sun refused to rise. "I remember the Legion. It's what they call themselves. Their army."

The word spoke of the monumental dead, of souls that were centuries old, of soldiers marching forward in a war more horrifying than I could ever imagine.

Legion. The Grand Army of the Dead.

Abby's grandmother walked over to her and took her hand. "Dear, this is silliness. It's just your coma talking. Your mind was in and out. We nearly lost you —"

"That's when my mother came to me!" Abby said fiercely. "She came to the hospital!"

"Oh, Abby," said Grammy Nora. Her eyes pooled with tears.

"The Legion is coming here, soldier by soldier," said Ronny, still staring off into the distance. "It's evil against good. Evil is winning."

"But Abby," Grammy Nora said. "Dear, this is —"

Abby took her grandmother by the shoulders. "Grammy, no! He's right. They're both right. I heard it in my coma, only I didn't want to believe it. People are coming. Dead people."

The old woman paled, shocked by Abby's insistence, her flashing eyes and darkening features.

Finally, she nodded. "Yes . . . okay . . ." she stammered. "I believe you, Abby. But what are we supposed to do? What can we hope to —"

"Don't hope," Ronny snarled, more darkly than I'd ever heard him before. "There's no time for hope. Just run. Hide." He turned to me. "Derek, we have to go to Bayou Malpierre. Now. Maybe your father — our father — can tell us what to do next."

"Come, dear," said Grammy Nora, pulling Abby toward the car.

Abby looked at me. Ronny was already walking away.

"Good-bye," she said. "I don't know . . ."

I could tell her mind was racing. She was struggling to uncover things she hadn't remembered yet. They would haunt her until she did.

Like me and Ronny, she knew something we needed.

"Here's my cell number," I said, writing it down for her on a scrap of paper. "Call me if you remember anything else."

Grammy Nora put her arm around Abby and helped her back into the car.

As I watched them drive away, I hoped I'd see Abby again. But Ronny had just warned us against hope. So never mind. We had to go.

"Let's find my car," Ronny called over his shoulder. "Come on."

EIGHT

The Roof Angel

The day was still hazy but already burning hot as we headed into the Quarter. We knew Ronny's car was parked in the alley behind our house. We didn't know if it would still be drivable. We hadn't seen it since the fire.

"I hate this place," Ronny grumbled when we turned onto Royal Street. "I'll sneak around back and bring out the car. Stay hidden."

"Be careful —" I said, but he was already out of earshot. I let him go. He was hardly Ronny much anymore. The War had changed Virgil Black. Coming back had changed him, was changing him, every day he stayed here.

I was changing, too.

It was too much to think about. I was back in the Quarter for the first time in a day, staring at the ruins of the house that I'd lived in my whole life. The bottom story was charred, the front door and windows busted through and boarded up. The firefighters probably did that. The old red brick was stained with soot. It shot upward from the windows, like the ragged wings of a giant raven.

My eyes followed the burn marks up to the top floor and then to the *faux chambre* at the very top of the house. Dad's special room. Why my eyes were drawn to the angel ornament on the peak, I couldn't tell you, but my heart quickened with the sudden words that popped into my head.

I was . . . an angel child . . . child of light . . .

The ornament had survived the fire, but its wings and face were black with soot.

I watched a lone fireman walk gingerly across the roof. He carried an ax in his hand and peered in the broken windows of the secret room. He pulled away, then stomped his feet on the rooftop, answered the walkie-talkie on his belt, and stomped some more.

On top of my burned house.

The word *Legion* echoed in my head, like a pebble dropped in a steel drum. The Legion had destroyed my family, taken my house, forced me to run.

Don't hope? Just run and hide?

Would the Legion ever stop chasing us? Why should they? They needed people to die, so they would have more bodies to translate into. They fought me and Ronny because we knew about them. So I was on the run. It was more than that, but how much more, I didn't know.

Twice I turned away from my blackened house. Twice I turned back. Twice I stared at that charred angel and knew I had to have it.

I had to have it.

The fireman was out of sight now. In seconds, I was across the street. I knew the building on the corner had a fire escape on the side street, so I used it. I pulled my heavy body up to the roof and crossed over to the far side. It was a short, clumsy jump to the next roof, and the next, and then to mine.

I glanced around. Still no fireman.

I moved over to the *faux chambre* and peered in the windows. Burned books and old model trains were scattered everywhere across the wet, blackened floor. I wanted to cry. But there was no time. I eased myself onto the hidden room's roof from behind, afraid it wouldn't hold me, but not about to stop now. With one quick swipe, I grabbed on to the burned figure. It was five and a half inches of carved, gilded wood, now blackened by ash.

What I was going to do with the thing, I couldn't tell you. But the moment I held it, I felt totally, completely sure that this was right. Having the angel with me was right.

I unscrewed it from its base and stuffed it in the

side pocket of my cargo pants. I slid back down to the main roof and stood there, breathing heavily. You'd think I'd just run a race or something.

"So there, Legion," I said.

It probably wasn't my most mature moment. So what?

That word — Legion — coiled in my left ear like metal twisting, screeching, squealing. It was the same sound I'd heard in the hospital. I shook my head to clear it, but the sound didn't fade.

I pressed my finger on my ear to block the sound, but only changed it to a kind of high-pitched hissing.

"What *is* that?" I said aloud.

Suddenly, a window shattered in the little room, spraying me with shards of glass.

I screamed. She was standing in the room. Cane's wife. Abby's mother. Her hand had thrust through the glass at me. The smell of something rotting hit me like a wave. It was awful, like old meat or garbage.

"Get away!" I yelled, tripping over my own feet and landing on my back. Her face was gray and horrible, her eyes filthy, staring through me.

"First . . ." she hissed. *"Firssssst . . ."* It was the same word she had said at the diner near Bordelon Gap.

Her eyes bored into mine. Her head twitched back and forth, stringy hair dripping over her sunken cheeks. My ear felt like it was being skewered. I finally crawled to my feet, tripped, doubled over, and turned to the roof's edge.

Firssssst . . .

I got over to the next roof, and the next, and the next, and onto the fire escape, tripping and stumbling but not stopping until I was on the ground again. The shrieking stayed in my head.

"Stop!" I groaned, slapping my hands over my ears.

"Quiet down!" Ronny said, running up the sidewalk toward me. "Are you crazy? What are you doing?"

"Her!" I spat. I told him everything, wobbling on my feet.

He made a noise in his throat. "Cane's wife? In our house?" Ronny's face twisted. He spun on his heels, clutching my arm to keep me from falling over. "This is worse than I thought."

NINE

Driving

I staggered down the street next to Ronny. "How could she get into our house in the first place?" I asked.

"She's dead," he said, tugging on my arm.

"What was she doing there?"

"I don't know. Hurry up. I got a car."

"Your car's okay?" I asked.

Ronny snorted angrily. "No. It's not even there. It must have been destroyed, because the pavement where I left it is burned black. I found another car."

He slipped into an alley, turned left, then quickly headed on for two blocks. I could barely keep up. Ronny stepped over to an older sedan, pulled a set of keys from his pocket, unlocked the door, slid into the driver's seat, and pushed the passenger door open.

"Get in," he said.

I did. Ronny started the car. We roared to the end of the block and sped out of the Quarter.

"Ronny, did we just steal this car?"

"Borrowed," he said.

"Borrowed?" I repeated. "From who?"

"From her," he said. "Sam . . . Samantha."

"What? Your old girlfriend?" I asked. The last time Ronny had seen her, she had left in tears.

"The car was parked on the street behind her house. I remembered that she always kept her keys in it." He breezed around a corner.

"You remember that?" I said. "That Samantha left the keys in her car? Really? That's Ronny stuff. There's still some of you left!"

"It's a mess in here," he said, tapping his forehead.

I knew that, of course. But I also liked knowing that Ronny — my brother — was still in there somewhere.

I suddenly caught a whiff of something bad, and I guessed that some critter had crawled under Sam's backseat and died there. How long had it been since she had even used the car? It struck me that Ronny needed to call Sam and tell her that we "borrowed" her car, so she wouldn't file a police report. We didn't have time for the police.

Ronny agreed, so I dialed the number and put my cell on speakerphone.

"Hello?" a voice answered. "Derek?"

"No. This is Vir — Ronny," Ronny said.

A pause. "Oh. Hi."

"Uh," he said, "I took your car."

"What?" Sam said.

"Borrowed. I borrowed your car. We need it. Me and Derek. For a little while. I'll bring it back later. I promise."

There was silence, then Sam said, "Take your time, Ronny. I know you're sorting some things out. I don't need the car right now. My dad can . . . Just take your time. The tires are a little low. Be safe."

Ronny stared at the phone. His eyes started to well up. I couldn't tell what was going through his mind, but the last thing I needed was for him to be crying at the wheel. I turned off the speaker and held the phone to my good ear.

"Thanks, Sam," I said. "Ronny says thanks."

"Okay," she replied sadly. "Take care of him, Derek, okay? Bye."

As I hung up, Ronny groaned under his breath and set his eyes firmly on the road. It hurt to hear how much Sam missed him. Even I could tell that. They had been close, but since he came back, Ronny had been so cold. He treated her as if he didn't know her. Which he kind of didn't.

Should I have told Sam what was actually going on? Translation? The Rift? The walking dead? Ronny and Virgil?

No. Sam was normal. A nice person. She wasn't in this, not like us. Not even like Abby.

At least having the car bought us some time. I just didn't know how much. Between the streetcar incident, the fire, and the hospital, the police had to know that something weird was happening. I mean, someone must have noticed how everyone who "died" in the train crash was suddenly around again. Or they would notice it soon.

If the police dragged me and Ronny back to New Orleans, the fight would be over. We'd never be able to explain things in a way that anyone would believe. Not to mention that they'd do tests on Ronny and realize he was, uh, not really alive.

Total freak show.

No. We had to keep moving.

The smell was getting worse in the heat, so I reached back and opened the rear windows of the car. The air was hot and wet, but at least it moved.

We were deep in morning traffic when my cell phone rang. The sound of Abby's voice on the other end sent a shiver through me. And not a bad shiver, either.

Ronny was watching me.

I pointed to the road ahead.

"I . . . remember something else," Abby said.

There were people talking in the background on her end. I wondered where she was.

"My mom told me something about the house," she said. "Not the one we saw, but that reminded me. She said something about a red house."

A red house. That didn't do anything for me. "Where is it?"

"I don't know," Abby said. "But I think the Legion is trying to find something. And maybe it's this house, wherever it is. I'll call you if I remember more."

There was yelling in the background now.

"What's going on?" I asked. "Where are you?"

"Home." She paused. "The police are here. They said that the morning after the train accident, the rescue crews spotted my mom —"

Oh, no. "What?"

"Her body, on the rocks," Abby said. "Far down the chasm."

On the rocks. That's where Ronny said he had died.

"But when the last search crew got down there, she wasn't there. They're saying the body must have fallen into the river and got washed away. Grammy is having a fit."

Should I tell her now? "Abby —"

"Nice, huh? I gotta go."

Before I could say anything, she hung up.

How long would it be before Abby learned the whole truth? There would be no way to sugarcoat it. Her mother died. Then she . . . *un*died.

About an hour southeast of New Orleans, as we were driving along the highway, Ronny turned to me.

"Listen," he said, "did you and Ronny . . . I mean . . . were you friends? Besides being brothers?"

Where did that come from?

"I had friends back in Shongaloo," he added.

Shongaloo. That word conjured up what I imagined Virgil Black's life had been like in 1938, before he died. He'd actually *had* a life. He'd had friends. I could only imagine what a mess all this was in his head. He was probably hoping to sort it out.

I tried to think of how to answer, but I couldn't. It was all too much. "Yeah, Ronny and I were friends. But that's over now," I said. "I just want to find Dad and try to make everything stop."

Ronny nodded, said, "That's fine," and went quiet.

My throat burned. I hated shooting him down, knowing that there might not be another moment like this one. But I also hated that Ronny was gone.

I didn't want to talk.

When a state police cruiser roared past us, I realized it was the third one I'd seen. We decided to get off the highway and take local roads from then on.

The day was sopping wet and burning hot, even through an overcast sky. It was just after noon when the land thinned out and the wetlands began.

Focusing as far off in the hazy distance as I could, I saw a dark mist rising off the waters that leaked into the Gulf of Mexico.

My chest ached. I was here again.

Bayou Malpierre.

TEN

Mist off the Water

Ronny slowed the car and suddenly pulled off the road. Other than some distant clumps of trees, there was nothing but flatland around us. Without the breeze, that awful odor filled the car again. The same smell from the roof of my house. The same smell as Cane's wife.

"What's the matter?" I asked.

Ronny held his index finger in front of his face, staring at it. It was the finger he had almost cut off while shaving. The tape I had used to bandage it was black with grime.

"What about it?" I said.

He raised the finger to his nose. "It took me a couple of hours to figure it out," he said. "This is what stinks." He peeled the soiled tape off, and I sucked in a gasp.

His fingertip was just as black as the bandage.

Taking the tip into his other hand, he twisted it

slowly until, with a sound like Velcro ripping, it broke off.

"Ronny! Oh, gawww —"

Turning the nib in front of his eyes, Ronny said, "How long am I going to be here? What's next, do you think? An ear? A foot?"

I didn't know how to answer.

He looked at me. "I sometimes wonder — did I ask to come back here? Did I volunteer to keep fighting? Because I don't even know. I don't want to be here."

I swallowed. It barely went down. "I'm glad you came back," I said quietly.

"I wish I'd never left Shongaloo."

"I know," I said. "But I'm glad you're here. With me."

He dropped his eyes and nodded. "That's it, then."

Ronny held the blackened tip of his finger for a minute, staring at it. Then he tossed it out the window, shoved the car in gear, and raced off.

My mind raced, too. What *would* happen to Ronny? Was he falling apart? What would be next? Why did his dead finger smell the same as Cane's mad wife? She died *on the rocks*. So did Ronny. Did that mean anything? Why didn't the others smell like that?

I had no answers.

We drove another half hour in silence. The heat was making me sleepy, until Ronny swerved the wheel. We rolled into a thickness of live oak and hunched cypress trees, all heavy with vines and wet moss.

Bayou Malpierre was a small area off the tail end of the Atchafalaya, a tributary of the Mississippi River. For centuries, the Atchafalaya's spillover had driven into the shallow land and flooded it. It had been overgrown and overcrowded by a forest of cypress and oak trees, moss and mangroves, vines and every kind of swampy vegetation you could imagine.

The deeper we went into it, the more forest grew around us. Soon it closed out the hazy sky altogether. Moving into the bayou was like falling into a place that hadn't changed for a hundred years. A thousand. A million.

Webs of green-black moss hung in tatters from cracked and bowed branches. All around us, sodden tree trunks grew out of — and died back into — pools of oil-dark water.

Something flashed across my mind. A memory. A place.

Five trees, broken and bent, stood in a half circle. Their thick limbs crisscrossed one another to form a kind of natural vault over a clearing that spread out on the soggy ground like an altar. Was that here? In Bayou Malpierre?

Would I see it again? What did it mean?

Ronny swerved the car quickly to avoid a tree stump, then plunged into a tunnel of low trees without slowing down.

"Careful!" I yelped. "It's not a tractor, you know!"

The squeal of branches scraping the car on both sides sent a chill up my spine. I hoped Sam would forgive us for making such a mess of her car.

Hope. That word again.

But that was the old Derek thinking. A banged-up car would mean less than nothing in a war against the dead. So skip it. Keep going.

Soon, we found ourselves on a narrow, rutted path. The tree branches hung low, scraping the car roof.

"We can't drive anymore," Ronny said, stepping on the brake.

When he cut the engine, we heard rumbling far off among the trees. It came from somewhere beyond what we could see.

"Come on," Ronny said. He climbed out of the car, slammed the door, and shoved the keys into his pocket.

We made sure the car was mostly hidden, then slowly pressed forward through the jungle. No more than half a mile later, I was surprised to see three open flatboats motoring slowly out behind a levee, a continuous mound of earth designed to protect lowlands from flooding.

"Look at them," I said, stopping to watch.

Ronny eyed the boats, saying nothing.

Each of the boats had fifteen or twenty passengers crowded against the railing. They were all in cargo shorts and wore sun hats and dark glasses. It seemed like they were having some kind of party. Some held cameras, others leaned over and dipped their hands into the water.

"Tourists," I said, "heading into the bayou for a happy ride among the wonders of nature."

"Uh-huh," Ronny grunted.

I hated the bayou. Dreaded it. But as laughter rolled across the water, I found myself feeling comforted by the sight of real people enjoying themselves. These tourists, acting so normal, made me feel oddly hopeful, as if we had left all the craziness back in New Orleans. As if those wild streets, the haunted cemetery, the dark alleys, the marching dead, would just stay back there.

As if the rising of the dead was a city thing.

Then Ronny scowled. "How nice for them to know nothing about a horror they could never imagine anyway."

My small sense of hope shriveled up and died.

The tour boats moved on, the sound of the motors faded, and I felt alone again.

"Let's keep moving," said Ronny.

Before long we saw a house, if you can call it that. The place was only a little larger than a doghouse, but less well built, on a narrow spit of land nearly surrounded by stagnant green water. It was basically a shack of four walls topped by a corrugated tin roof, higher on one side than the other like a shed. The whole thing was perched seven or eight feet above the sodden ground on posts that looked like hen's feet.

"Chicken shack," said Ronny.

"I'll say."

Ronny looked at me funny. "No, I mean it's actually a chicken shack. I used to build those in Shongaloo."

Virgil again.

I saw flies buzzing in and out of the single open window. Maybe there was discarded food inside. Maybe even a corpse. It made my throat thicken to think about it. A filthy shack, in the middle of nowhere with unspeakable insides.

But the more I stared at it, the more the feeling haunted me that this wasn't the first time I had seen the place. I felt the heavy spell of the swamp fall on me.

"I've been here before," I said.

"Lucky you," said Ronny dryly.

A boat horn echoed harshly across the open water.

I turned. "What is –"

Suddenly, an airboat – an aluminum flatboat with a giant propeller fan spinning in the rear – soared over the side of the levee, coiled through the air, and slammed to the ground, headed right for us.

ELEVEN

Finding What's Missing

The airboat shuddered to a stop a foot away from me. The propeller blades whirred to a standstill. Quiet fell over the bayou.

I really didn't need the added drama of almost being run over.

The airboat's driver said nothing. He was a man about my father's age, dressed in a T-shirt, grimy overalls, and a ragged baseball cap. He narrowed his eyes at me and Ronny, then spit off the side of the airboat.

I didn't like the look of him. Even after nearly driving over us, he seemed so calmly planted to his seat. He just stared at us and said nothing.

Ronny and I waited.

"Is one of you boys Derek Stone?" the man asked finally.

Oh, boy. "Uh . . . "

"Who wants to know?" interrupted Ronny.

"If one of you is," the man went on, showing two missing teeth up front, "I'm Smitty Fouks. Most people call me Bonton. Your daddy asked me to leave some flowers at an old tomb in the city. He said you'd understand. If one of you's him, I guess you did. Your daddy'll be here by nightfall."

I took a step forward. "I'm Derek. My dad's really coming?"

The man eyed me up and down. "I said he was, didn't I?"

I didn't like the way he spat again after he said that.

He continued. "But first, Waldo's missing. Weather's uncertain. We got to find him. Climb on in."

Ronny held me back. "Who's Waldo?" he asked.

Bonton looked Ronny up and down. I wondered if he noticed his missing fingertip. "Waldo's my precious boy."

The words sounded odd.

"And?" said Ronny.

"Waldo wandered off," the man went on. "The bayou's like his own big, wet yard. He could be anywhere. I got to find him before it gets dark. There might be rain."

Ronny's cold hand was still on my arm, holding me back.

"Can you help me look?" Bonton pleaded, patting the seat next to him as if he expected us to jump right in.

I hated the water. I wanted to stay on land and wait for my father. Plus, this guy was like some crazy caricature. I didn't know whether to trust him.

"Waldo's out there," he said, peering into the trees.

I glanced at Ronny. He shared my look. I guess we both silently agreed that if Dad wasn't coming until later, there was no reason not to help Bonton. Dad knew him, after all. What else were we going to do?

So Ronny and I climbed into the airboat and strapped in next to the man. He spit a third time and pushed a green button with his thumb. The propellers roared behind us.

"Hold on!" he hollered.

I was thrown back in my seat when we shot off the wet ground and hit the water. As the boat bounced along, I remembered just how much I hated the bayou.

We drove under a tangled cascade of vines and into a slightly broader, weaving waterway, picking up speed with every moment. Soon we came upon the tour boats Ronny and I had seen earlier. Now the passengers were singing to recorded music.

Bonton growled as we passed. "City folk, hoping

to catch a glimpse of the glory of the bayou. They don't know anything about it. Waldo laughs when the guides tell those people wrong things. He's a seer, Waldo is."

"A seer?" I said. "What do you mean?"

Bonton drove fast, and wind blew in our faces, stifling our words. He turned to look at me, then banked left out of the main waterway into a denser system of coiling tributaries. He cut the engine to a lower speed.

"My precious boy sees things before they happen," he said. "He knows things that the rest of us don't. Six years ago, during the big flood, that's when he got his insight. He loves this here bayou. Never been out of it. Of course, being a seer doesn't always help him know where he's going all the time. Some days, he just gets lost."

If I wasn't sure about Bonton, I really wasn't sure about his precious Waldo. Was Dad really friends with this guy? And why did we have to meet here? Dad knew how much I hated this place.

Bonton eased the airboat deeper into the swamp, among the massive trunks and tiny islands. He steered with one hand, shifting, pedaling the brake, and throttling through the tall reeds. I glanced at Ronny. I could tell he hadn't made up his mind about the man yet, either. I asked Bonton how he knew my father.

"Your daddy and me go way back," he said in a slow drawl. "I've lived in the bayou forever. He sold me three boats over the years. I only have this one left. He took a shine to my precious little boy, too."

That word was getting on my nerves. Ronny snorted and looked away.

"Your daddy'd stop here every few months to check on me and my boats, and he'd bring a little toy for Waldo. My boy sure loves those trains."

Trains?

In my mind I saw the scattered, broken, burned trains in my father's rooftop study. Then I pictured Abby's dead mother reaching for me, and the wooden angel in my pants pocket.

"What trains?" I asked, even though I knew.

"Your daddy brought him toy trains."

I felt ashamed that Dad had found someone who appreciated his love of trains more than Ronny and I did.

"Nice," I said. I didn't mean it.

Bonton went quiet as we reentered the waterway and circled into the swamp a second time. Nearly an hour had gone by and the sky was darkening with clouds. Fifty feet to our left, we could see more of the levee that Ronny and I had passed earlier. The earthen wall was ten or twelve feet high at this point.

It looked like an enormous grassy snake, slumbering in the water and nearly buried by dense tree cover.

"Every few years, when there were heavy rains, the bayou would flood," Bonton said, keeping his eyes fixed on the crest of the earth wall. "So we got a brand new dike, to ease excess water into the bayou nice and slow. You understand?"

"Like a lock," said Ronny. "It regulates the flow of water."

"That's right," said Bonton. "In a little moment, you'll see our very own lock gate!"

As we drifted along the levee, I followed it with my eyes to where the wall was interrupted by two thick cement posts, each about three feet wide. Between the posts was an iron slab divided in the middle. It looked like a set of dungeon doors. Something moved there, on top of the wall.

Bonton shouted, "There he is! Waldo!" He shut off the engine. "I should have known! That boy loves our new dike. He likes to dangle his toes in the deep side. Say, Waldo!"

I saw the boy clearly now, sitting on top of the iron slab. He was a little figure in green overalls and no shirt, facing away from us. He looked about six years old at most, with blond curls all the way to his shoulders. I could see why his father called him his "precious" boy. From behind, he looked like a cherub in overalls. And he seemed to be talking to someone I couldn't see.

"Waldo!" Bonton called. "Hey, Ralph Waldo Fouks!"

So that was his name? Weird.

The boy did not turn when his father called.

"How old is Waldo?" asked Ronny.

"Eleven," Bonton said.

Eleven! My eyes went wide. Waldo looked no more than five or six.

"Is he talking to someone on the other side?" I asked.

"No one to talk to out here," said Bonton. "He's just deep in himself. He's like that sometimes."

We drifted as close to the wall as we could. I watched Waldo's hand moving back and forth across the top of the metal slab. As we neared, I saw a toy train in his hand.

"Choo! Choo-choo!"

"Silly boy," said Bonton, grinning. "He doesn't even sense the danger of sitting on that dike. This bayou's fed by the Atchafalaya River and the Red River before that. The Red River can rile up fierce in a sudden rain."

Ronny leaned toward me. "You know where else the Red River runs?" he whispered.

My heart skipped a beat. Of course I did. "Bordelon Gap."

Bonton cupped his hands around his mouth and called up to the tiny boy. "Waldo! Waldo . . ."

The little figure stiffened, then turned slowly. Waldo was definitely small for his age, there was no doubt about that. But his face was — I don't even know how to say it.

Precious boy?

I couldn't imagine a brighter, happier face, especially out here in the sticks. Waldo's cheeks were pink, his eyes wide, and he had a great big smile on his lips.

"Poppa Bonton!" he said with a warm laugh. "But you aren't alone, are you, Poppa?" His voice was soft and melodic, as if he were reciting a poem. "Is that Derek Stone with you?"

Ice ran through my veins. I shook it off.

"I bet it is!" Waldo went on. "Derek! I'm happy to meet you!"

Ronny made a noise under his breath, but me — I don't know why — I couldn't help but smile at the precious boy.

"Happy to meet you, too," I said.

TWELVE

Little Boy Down

Bonton kept his eyes on his son while he spoke to us. "Would you boys mind . . ." He pointed to the levee and trailed off.

"You want us to help him down?" asked Ronny.

"It's my leg," Bonton explained, slapping his left thigh. I noticed that his leg was crooked and several inches shorter than the right one. It ended in a large black boot. "I broke it in three places during that old flood. It only healed in two. Plus, this here foot's not even real!"

He slapped the thick prosthetic boot. It made a hollow sound, and I couldn't help shivering. I needed to toughen up.

"I guess," I said, though I had no idea how to get up a twelve-foot-high embankment. I wondered how little Waldo had climbed up there in the first place.

Ronny and I jumped down to a narrow path running along the earthen wall. Ronny did all right getting up the levee, but it wasn't an easy climb for me. Twelve feet is higher than you think. Especially when you're hauling extra weight and are terrified of water. Bonton kept offering Waldo encouragement, telling him not to worry, help was on the way. I wanted him to throw a little of that encouragement my way, but I wasn't about to say that.

The boy had been quiet during our climb, but when we came close, he hooted, "Chugga-chugga-choo!"

Then he laughed. It sounded like the jangling of tiny bells. The closer I got, the more I could see that Waldo was a lot like a feather — frail and thin. He looked like a foundling or an orphan, the way his too-long overalls were cuffed up to his knees.

"They're coming, Waldo," called Bonton. "Soon now!"

Waldo smiled. "I'm being rescued!"

As I worked my way slowly across the top of the wall, I discovered that even though the water level on the bayou side was low, the water on the far side lapped all the way up to Waldo's dangling, shoeless feet.

Waldo turned his bright little face right to me, his hair a golden waterfall. I'll never forget it. Dabbed on his rosy cheeks were what looked like grains of powder, and his lips were red, but only in the center, as if he'd been eating berries.

But as odd as that was, my heart skipped when I looked into Waldo's eyes. From a distance, they had seemed radiant, sparkling. Up close, his eyes were blank, empty, and fixed on the distance over my shoulder. They didn't move at all.

Waldo was blind.

Ronny saw it, too, and gasped. "You can't . . . see . . ." he stammered.

"I know what you're thinking," Waldo said. "And it's true. I'm blind as a bat!" I looked down at the water, and my legs tingled. *Get it together, Derek.*

"So how did you get all the way up here?" I asked, focusing on the boy to distract myself.

Waldo smiled shyly. "I know my bayou, every inch of it. I feel like I've known it for a hundred years. More!"

I noticed then that his teeth were tiny little nibs. Baby teeth? Waldo was eleven years old with baby teeth? I shuddered a little.

"Home, Waldo?" Bonton hollered from below us.

"Yes, Poppa!" Waldo went on. "But let's not forget my rowboat. It's right . . . there!" He swiveled slowly and pointed away from us, as if he could see with his blank eyes. Right where he pointed was a beat-up little boat, tethered to a stump on the shallow side of the levee. Bonton chuckled, limped along the levee path, dragged the rowboat to his airboat, and tied it fast as we climbed back down to the airboat. Waldo was amazingly surefooted for a little kid who couldn't see. I tried not to let him show me up, even though I kept picturing myself tumbling down into the murky bayou of my nightmares.

Once we'd all made it back to the boat, Waldo said, "Now, home!"

Bonton motored up and turned the airboat around.

"Are we in the waterway now, Poppa?" Waldo asked, sniffing the air.

"You guessed it, son," said Bonton.

Waldo looked at me with his blank eyes. "Some places, the water gets deep," he said. "I hear tour guides say ten feet. That's not right. Thirty, fifty feet, even more in some places, even this side of the levee. Some places go all the way down —"

"All the way down?" asked Ronny. "To what?"

Waldo's little face beamed. "To . . . whatever!"

I felt like my atoms were spinning out of control, and I'd scatter into a trillion pieces. I tried to focus on seeing Dad soon, but couldn't. Why did he choose this faraway place to meet us, anyway? Everything about it creeped me out.

As we turned into the swamp near the shack, Waldo jumped in the seat next to me. "Look there, Derek!" he said. "Look!"

About a hundred feet away, nearly buried by a mess of vines and growth that kept me from seeing it before, were the remains of an ancient cemetery.

Its tombs were half submerged. Set in little streets like the cemeteries back home, the crypts were broken, crumbling into the black water. Their pitted white stone was blackened by mold.

"That boneyard's a hundred fifty, two hundred years old," said Bonton. "Used to be on dry land, but that's the way things go in Malpierre. Down and down and, finally, down. The bayou keeps getting deeper, breathing, like it's alive."

If they stood at all, the old tombs stood only because they leaned on their neighbors. Dark water lapped halfway up the crypts' doors, many of which had cracked open. Waves washed inside the resting places. My stomach turned.

I shivered. "The bodies . . ."

"Are where the bayou takes them!" said Waldo cheerfully.

I imagined the open stone cases. The waterlogged bodies. The water moving over them.

We motored slowly past the Venice of the dead, frozen as it collapsed. I wanted to turn away. Waldo kept his face on it for as long as he could, though, as if his blank eyes could see.

When we reached the shack, Bonton parked the airboat with the rowboat in tow, and we climbed down.

At once, Waldo froze in place, thrust his head toward the sky, and whooped loudly.

"Waldo, are you seeing something again?" asked Bonton.

"I'm feeling it, Poppa," said the boy, his face jerking one way then the other. "The rain!"

Even before he finished laughing, the sky cracked open. It began to pour.

THIRTEEN

In the Shack

A gash of lightning sliced across the haze. Rain came down like bullets. The air turned black.

We hurled ourselves up the shaky steps and into Bonton's shack seconds before a second bolt of lightning crashed overhead.

Being in the shack's single room was hardly better than being outside. The rain battered the roof like gunshots — *bang-bang-bang!* — causing leaks in a dozen places. Just like in the old house in New Orleans, the floor was soaked.

But the strangest part was watching Waldo.

He stayed out in the rain longer than the rest of us and came in sopping wet. Then he moved across the room with his hands out, not to feel his way around, but to find where water was dripping from the ceiling. Once he found a place that poured like a spout, he giggled, sat down under it, and turned his face up into the little stream. The water dripped from his forehead to his chin, streaking his cheeks. Again, his laugh was like bells.

I shared a look with Ronny. "That's normal," he whispered, making a face.

All the while, Bonton's eyes never left his son. He never stopped smiling. "What a child!"

"So, when do you think my dad will come?" I asked over the pounding rain, trying to get back on track. I didn't like the way Bonton shook his head.

"I had said soon, but after sunset's always a hard time to enter the bayou," he said with a snort. "Double, when it storms. Easy to get lost. We wrap ourselves in at night, don't we, Waldo?"

"Yes, sir!" said the boy brightly, fluttering his eyelids into the sputtering raindrops. "And it's looking like a you-know-what kind of night!"

"What kind of night is that?" Ronny asked warily.

I wasn't sure I wanted to know.

Bonton winked at his blind son, who, oddly, appeared to wink back. Maybe it was just a blink. "Waldo, how about you favor us with the story?"

Waldo nodded. "Surely, Poppa." He opened his mouth to the rain once more, then shifted over to Ronny and me.

"On a rainy night in the bayou, you might see her.

You might see *Bellamina*." He paused, waiting for us to react.

We took the bait.

"Bellamina?" Ronny said.

"Who's she?" I asked.

"*She* is a *what*!" said Waldo gleefully. "*Bellamina*'s a big old steamboat!"

"From a time long forgotten, except in these parts," added his father. "A hundred and fifty years ago or more —"

"More!" Waldo said, as the rain pounded harder. "*Bellamina* was a side-wheeler, painted black from her hull all the way to her top deck. She could sneak around without anybody seeing her. But me? I saw her!"

Bonton's eyebrows shot up. "You saw her?"

"No, that was a lie," said Waldo quickly. "I never saw her. But *Bellamina* went all up and down the Atchafalaya. She was the floating home of a gang of smugglers! Oh, they were bad. They did away with folks who got in their way. Their captain —"

"Oh, now, I don't like this part," Bonton cut in, shaking his head quickly. He limped over to the door, looked out at the battering rain, then closed the door more tightly. "But you tell it, Waldo. You tell it."

"Their captain was a murderer," the boy went on,

his voice lowering, "and a poor cripple who never left his boat. The *Bellamina,* she was the terror of the Atchafalaya for years. But she was never caught, until one night a flash flood drove her into Malpierre. Drove her right here!"

Waldo moved his hands around him as if smoothing an invisible tablecloth. "And she sank, the *Bellamina* did. The crew would follow their captain anywhere. He couldn't leave his boat, so neither did they. They died on it. Folks say that every time it rains, the *Bellamina* could rise again. I bet we'll know it when she does."

"How?" Ronny asked. Thunder clapped outside, loud and booming.

Waldo kept smiling in my direction. "Because of the dogs! The captain kept a pack of dogs. They were wild, but they'd obey him. Dogs, Derek."

Dogs, Derek?

Did Waldo know about the dogs that chased me?

"They say that when the *Bellamina* sank, the dogs were hunting on shore, separated from their master," said Waldo, his voice lowering even more. "They starved and died here. They've haunted the bayou ever since. They'll howl when she rises again!"

The boy paused, almost as if he were waiting for someone to speak. No one did, until Bonton wobbled to the door a second time. He cracked it open and peered out while rain blew in on us. "That black boat can't rise anymore," he said. "Not since they built that lock. Malpierre's not deep enough now to float anything that big."

Waldo opened his mouth to drink the water dripping from the ceiling, and giggled like bells again. "It sure isn't," he said. Then he stiffened, letting the rainwater pour down his chin. "Oh, Poppa!" he called, turning to the door.

"Yes, Waldo, what is it?" Bonton asked.

"I see . . . water. Dark water. And —" Waldo grasped my arm tightly. "It's coming!"

I wanted to shake the boy's hand loose, but an alarm shrieked in the distance and echoed through the dense trees.

Bonton pushed past me and looked out into the rain. "No, no," he said.

"What is it?" I asked.

"That's the alarm bell at the lock," Bonton explained hurriedly. "One of the levees upriver has been breached. Maybe more than one. The river's gonna be wild. There could be a flood coming our way!"

I looked at Ronny. Ronny looked at Bonton. Bonton looked at Waldo who, swallowing more rainwater, began to laugh.

FOURTEEN

It Begins

Everything happened at once. Thunder crashed like bombs, followed by the faraway sound of splintering wood. The house shook on its peg legs. Bonton hobbled on his one real leg like a man possessed. "Thanks to you, Waldo, we'll have time to warn those tour boats!" he cried. "Malpierre surges in a flood. Those drivers need to know the safe way out. Derek, Ronny, come with me. Waldo, you stay here!"

"Yes, Poppa," the boy said calmly. "You know I will."

While the shack trembled like a shoebox on toothpicks, Bonton hopped down the stairs to the airboat.

Ronny followed him out into the rain. "Derek!" he called back to me.

I lurched to the door, but Waldo's fingers were still wrapped around my wrist. "Don't leave me, Derek, I'm scared!"

"Derek!" Ronny shouted. "Come on —"

"Hold on!" I yelled back.

The sky thundered again and again.

"We have to go!" called Bonton, his voice receding.

"Ronny! Ronny!" I yelled, making my way to the door and dragging Waldo with me. I struggled to keep the door open. Wind and rain whipped my face, while Waldo clung to my wrist. He wasn't letting go. His blank eyes searched my face. It was almost like he was trying to read my thoughts.

The airboat's engine roared over the sound of the storm.

"Ronny!" I called. "Don't leave me here!"

But the airboat disappeared into the bayou.

"The water's rising, isn't it?" Waldo asked calmly, as a wave crashed against the pilings under the shack. "Just like I said it would. It was already deep behind the lock."

There was a sudden crack, and the floorboards split enough that I could see the water flooding beneath us. I fell and slid across the floor. Waldo managed to stay on his feet, still holding on to me.

"We need to get out of here!" I said. "The house will crumble with us inside it —"

Thunder crashed again. The walls shook.

"Yes, Derek," Waldo said, not easing his grip or showing any sign of panic.

I crawled to the door. The front steps had twisted off the little shack and were floating away, a crumpled mess. I yanked my wrist from Waldo's hands and dropped straight down into the water, trying not to think about it. It came halfway to my knees. Waldo jumped down next to me, and the water reached his waist. The rain pounded us heavily. I could barely see.

I took a step, slipped, steadied myself, and reached for the boy, but Waldo made a sudden noise and quickly scuttled away.

"Waldo!" I cried out.

I struggled after him. The rain came down like bullets on my face, arms, back. Vines whipped around madly in the wind. "Waldo! Get back here!" I yelled. The water was rising faster now. I couldn't tell where to step. Then I heard a cry. Or maybe a laugh. I saw Waldo climbing into his rowboat.

"Where are you going?" I called into the storm.

He didn't hear me, or didn't want to. Was he going to paddle his dumb little boat in this rainstorm? Where did he think he was going?

"Waldo!" I cried.

No answer. Only that strange laugh of his. I urged myself through the storm after him. It felt like pushing a statue through mud. I waded from tree to tree, water beyond my knees now, trying to keep his rowboat in sight. Then a voice called out from somewhere behind me.

I turned. The rain was deafening. This was why I hated the bayou. You never knew where you were.

"Ronny?" I yelled. "Over here!"

No answer.

I pushed toward where I had last seen the rowboat. My foot twisted. I fell to my knees on something hard and flat, and water rushed up around my waist. I shielded my eyes, rubbed the rain from them. All around me stood the angled shapes of those crumbling bone houses.

I was in the cemetery again. That sinking city of the dead.

A laugh echoed through the storm. There was Waldo, rowing his way among the half-submerged tombs, paddling through the stone houses.

Cold rain splattered my face. My ears froze. Or were they burning hot? I couldn't tell. My lungs ached with each breath. I heard the voice again.

I heard the voice, only . . .

What I heard wasn't a single voice. It was several voices. And they weren't human.

They were howling dogs.

"No . . . no . . ." I gasped.

Something moved among the dark trees. Three,

five, eight shapes. I sloshed as fast as I could between the tombs. The muddy ground sucked my shoes off.

Now I could see the dogs. Starved animals of bone and teeth, they were so emaciated they looked almost invisible. Where the rain struck them, it outlined their shapes, moving swiftly behind the tombs.

I tried to climb to the top of one crypt, but the rain poured off the stone sides and I kept slipping. The dogs were in the open now. As one, they splashed across the mushy ground, their heads fixed on me. They held their mouths wide, teeth struck by raindrops, gleaming in the dark.

I turned and ran, frantically thrusting my way between the tombs. Then I tripped and struck my forehead on a broken stone.

Blood in my eyes, I stood up, tried to get my bearings. The dogs were moving fast.

They leaped at me.

FIFTEEN

Under the Five Trees

A sudden shriek pierced the darkness.

The dogs slid silently to a halt. I scrambled backward, falling, getting up. Heavy raindrops washed over the dogs like watercolors.

Soon there was only the splattering, empty earth around me.

I wiped the blood from my eyes and staggered to my feet. Where had the dogs gone?

Where? That's when I realized where I was.

No longer in the boneyard's alleys, I had made my way to higher ground. I stood beneath a vault of trees — five drowned oaks, crisscrossed in a half circle.

And right there amid the broken trees, with rain dripping off his smiling face, water to his knees, and his empty rowboat behind him, was Waldo.

His blind eyes glistened like black marbles.

"Ghost dogs," he said. His voice was hollow, deeper than before. "I call them on. I call them off."

I tried to step back, but only slid to my knees in the muck.

"You're nuts," I said. It felt good to say it.

"Ten years ago," Waldo said, "you were here."

My heart pounded. "What are you talking about?"

"Ten years ago, you were drowning . . . *right here,*" he said, waving his hands around as if he knew exactly where he was.

"What do you know about that?" I spat.

"I know what drowning's like," he said. His voice sounded even lower now. "Water running up your nose, filling your ears, your mouth? You panic, don't you? I know I did."

Waldo didn't even sound like the precious boy anymore. His face was changing, too. His features were sinking into themselves. His long blond hair was matted, pasted to his cheeks like dark rivulets of oil. All the color I had first seen in his face had washed away. His skin was gray.

"Your lungs burn like they're on fire," he went on, "screaming at you to fill them with air. But you don't want to breathe in water. . . ."

I glanced around, trying not to panic, looking for a way out.

"I know what it feels like," Waldo said, "because I drowned here, too. Six summers ago. The only difference is, maybe you survived. I didn't."

The storm went silent in my head.

"You were . . . one of them," I whispered.

"I *am* one of them," he said quietly. "I . . . he was playing one day and slipped into the swamp. Underwater, as he sunk, he saw the *Bellamina,* and got trapped in its railing. Then he saw a face, the captain. Soon it was me swimming to the surface. I've been here for six years, trying to figure out how I could bring my crew back. To continue the war." Waldo paused a moment, then grinned. "To *win* the war."

A thundering crash sounded in the distance. I knew right away what it was — the lock gate had fallen. Water was going to rush through the bayou. Any minute.

I heard a shrill, electric squeal. The sound system on the tour boats. A moment later, a flare shot up overhead. It blossomed red and hung in the stormy sky.

"You did this," I hissed at Waldo, as the water rose nearly to my waist. "You did something at the lock. You want to sink the tourist boats!"

"I took the blind, broken body of this boy," Waldo retorted. "I waited a long time for the *Bellamina* to rise . . . for you to return to Malpierre."

"For me?" I said. "What are —"

"I came here to find out if you knew about the first."

I shivered. The word Mrs. Cane — Abby's mother — had used. *First.*

"I don't know what you're talking about," I yelled.

"Maybe," he said quietly. "Maybe not."

A voice rippled through the darkness. "Derek!"

Waldo twisted. His head rattled from side to side, like a paint can in a mixer. "I guess I'll have to wait," he said. "Someone's coming for you. Let's give him something to do."

"Here I am!" I cried out. My voice was drowned out by the battering rain. It sounded no louder than a whisper. The distant call was moving away.

"Help!" I choked. I could hardly hear myself.

"Why are you whispering?" asked Waldo, stepping toward me. "Afraid to wake the dead? It's too late for that."

"Help . . ." My voice was hoarse with fear.

"Sorry. I've got my own helping to do," Waldo said, moving closer. "I have to bring back my crew."

"I'll stop you," I said, trying to sound strong.

"You'll try," he replied.

Waldo's dead-eyed face grinned horribly at me. I clenched my fists to punch it.

I should have been watching his hand.

By the time I saw the train, it was too late. Waldo slammed the iron toy into the side of my head so quickly that I barely heard the crack of my skull before I fell into the water.

The swamp surrounded me. Dark water filled my mouth, my nose.

The bayou wanted me.

Again.

SIXTEEN

The Hand

I tried to claw to the surface, but you can't crawl up water. The weight of it pressed on my chest like a stone.

Water of birth, water of death, alone, alone, alone . . .

The sudden words made me angry, even as I brushed them out of my mind. Would anyone save me this time?

Cold white fingers clutched at me, cold hands. Was I seeing things? It didn't matter. No one was coming. Soon I would leak away.

Shapes flew around me like smoky figures rising, falling, reaching out with long fingers. Then, a face. Black hair moving around a pale face.

Who was it?

Fingers wrapped around my hand. I tried to pull away. The grip was too strong and wouldn't let go. Cold fingers on my forehead. I struggled against them. My lungs nearly gave out. The angel ornament in my pocket suddenly seemed heavy. It weighed me down. I sank.

Then my body doubled over in the water. I broke the surface. Air! A shape huddled over me, pumping my chest, slapping my cheeks.

"Derek, Derek, Derek!"

I blew out a lungful of water. I coughed up black muck, sucked air into my mouth, coughed, breathed. I saw a face. A face I loved.

"Dad!" I cried, clutching the arms of my father. His wet face dripped on mine. "Dad!"

"Don't talk, Derek," he said. "Breathe —"

"You saved me!" I said. "Again! In the same place."

He tipped my face to the side and pumped my chest. I coughed out more black water, nearly fainting, coughing, coming to again.

"You saved me. It was you, you did it again —"

"No!" he shouted. Dad shook his head. He helped me sit up on the lid of a crypt. "No, Derek. I was there that night, ten years ago. But it wasn't me. I didn't pull you from the water. I found you, but someone else saved you."

"Who?" I asked.

He kept shaking his head. "I don't know. Here in Malpierre, ten years ago, you saw something no one else saw."

"Dad, what are you saying?"

"We'll find out together," he said, helping me up. The words made me feel hope again. "Derek, we have to find him. The first one who was translated. The dead are coming here to find him."

Hadn't Abby told me her mother said that? They were trying to find someone?

"There's one secret to understanding all this," Dad said. "And I think it's in what you saw that night. Only you know. That's why you had to come back here, to remember that night."

I was breathless. "Why didn't you ever tell me? You knew all this, and you never told me?"

He didn't answer.

I started to shake. "Your hand, Dad."

"What?"

"Show me your left hand," I said.

Ever since I'd seen pieces of a hand at the Coroner's office, pieces whose DNA matched my father's, I had hoped that whatever was left of my father's hand wasn't black and rotten like Ronny's finger.

I had hoped. But I needed proof.

"I have to see it."

He didn't move. I grabbed his wrist and forced his hand from his pocket. It was a thickly bandaged lump. Spots of dried blood, brown and dull, showed through the grimy cloth.

"Unwrap it," I said. "I have to know what it looks like. Unwrap it."

"Derek —"

Screams burst through the rain. The tourists. Sudden sirens approached from the distance. I could hear the thunder of distant helicopters approaching.

"Waldo's bringing back the *Bellamina,*" I said, stumbling toward the lock, forgetting my injuries. "It's filled with dead souls. He's done this —"

Another scream broke through the storm. I recognized this one.

It was Ronny.

SEVENTEEN

Enemies

Dad and I tumbled into Waldo's empty rowboat. Rainwater in the bottom sloshed over our feet. My arms hurt, my head hurt, but I grabbed an oar, gave Dad the other one, and together we dug into the rising floodwater. We pushed our way among the trees toward the dike.

Finally, we spotted Ronny.

He stood, soaked and silent and staring into the trees on a small spit of land. The rise barely held itself up above the water.

I noticed Dad stiffen when he saw what had become of his other son. "Ronny!" he called.

We jumped out and ran to him, still clutching our oars like weapons. Ronny didn't move.

"Where's Bonton?" I asked him.

"Gone," Ronny mumbled. "We couldn't get to the boats. Then the dogs came. He ran."

There was a rustle among the trees. A shape moved out of the branches.

I stifled a scream.

It was Abby's mother.

"She found us," said Ronny. "They all found us."

So they were here, the dead from New Orleans. I couldn't understand how they got here so quickly, but it hardly mattered. They were everywhere I was.

The dead woman's eyes moved slowly from one to the other of us, then fixed on me. Her mouth opened and that sound like metal twisting, grinding like gears being stripped, slid into my bad ear.

I sank to my knees. "Stop!"

Was she going to speak again? Was she trying to speak to me? Had she actually been to the hospital to see Abby? Her dead eyes said nothing.

Instinctively, my father moved between the woman and me. Ronny helped me to my feet and shoved me behind him.

Abby's mother took a step forward, keeping her eyes on me. The branches rustled again, and another figure appeared. Erskine Cane.

I saw then how fierce the war in the afterlife had been.

Cane and Ronny stared at each other with so much hate, it was clear that their souls had battled long and hard. Poor Virgil, stuck in Ronny's slight form, while Cane was reborn in a monster body.

But Cane and this woman were part of the Legion, and we had to try to stop them.

The woman howled something incomprehensible and ran at me. I hated fighting her, knowing that she was in the body of Abby's mother. Anger took over, and I hurled the oar at her legs. She wailed and splashed onto the ground. She twitched, stared, tried to climb to her feet.

"Leave me alone!" I yelled.

Cane charged. But Ronny was quick. He had a chunk of tombstone in his hand and threw it at Cane, catching him in the face. Cane shouted and stumbled.

Cries echoed from across the swamp.

"We have to help the tourists!" Dad yelled. The three of us took off through the trees, with Cane and the woman after us. We sloshed through the mud and up to the crest of the levee, leaving them behind.

From there, we saw the first boat. Wave after wave rushed into the waterway so quickly that the boat had no time to maneuver. In moments, its bow was submerged and began to sink. Some passengers were thrown overboard, while others scrambled frantically up the deck to the rising stern. We ran along the levee toward them until a powerful rush of water barreled past, cutting us off. We watched helplessly as their boat heaved up and over, capsizing completely. The two other boats whirled into view now, struggling to stay afloat.

"What can we do?" I yelled.

"Over here!" Ronny shouted out to the closest tourists in the water. "Swim to the levee!"

Dad was furious. He slipped into the water and clawed his way back to the top of the levee, trying to find a way to reach the people. A sudden wave rammed the second boat into the upturned hull of the first. There was a flash, and the engine exploded. Fuel sprayed across its deck to the third boat.

A scream of sound pierced my ear — or was it a scream of light? Whatever it was, I saw a gash of white in the water, and my ear stung at the same time. It sounded like iron on iron, echoing until it ended in a shriek. It was like nothing I'd ever heard before.

"The Rift has opened!" Ronny shouted.

The water churned and heaved. Something from below was pushing it out of the way — the *Bellamina*.

It rose out of the water like a dead weight thrust up from below. The water sucked at it, pulling it back down, and yet it rose, inch by inch from the depths. A second explosion from the tour boats spilled burning fuel onto its drenched old decks.

The *Bellamina* was a great, horrible shape, black as night, dripping with smoking moss and burning vines and rotten weeds. Water poured off its sagging decks. It seemed ready to crumble in on itself, and yet it rose higher. Its broken, spokeless side-wheels turned and squealed, glistening in the battering rain. Soon the old boat was all we could see. It dwarfed the tiny tour boats.

Dark shapes moved against the sagging rails, from one deck to the next, all the way up to the peak. The rain dripped, crosshatching them, giving them shape, size, bulk.

"The dead souls of the smugglers," Ronny said under his breath.

Standing on top of the broken lock gate was the precious boy himself, Waldo, watching the scene he had made happen. His voice rose into a terrible bellow. "Boys, come and get 'em!"

Without pause, the shapes leaped from the *Bellamina*'s decks and dived at the tourists.

EIGHTEEN

The Old Black Boat

Ronny exploded in anger. "No, no, no!" Then he jumped off the levee, into the water.

"Ronny!" yelled Dad. "Get back here —"

But Ronny powered through the waves and reached the rising steamboat in moments. Grabbing a spoke of the side-wheel, he hoisted himself aboard. Then Dad jumped in too, swam underwater to the boat, and clambered onto the main deck.

I couldn't go in that water. I couldn't.

I watched as the last of the dead souls plunged into the churning waves. At first there was gargling, yelling, splashing, confusion. Then it was over.

The tourists rose from the depths.

Their faces gleamed in the firelight, gray, emotionless. The pastel-dressed women, the chubby bearded men, were now possessed by the dead. Their gray fingers clutched at the *Bellamina*'s hull. As they pulled themselves up on deck, one after another, I realized what I hadn't before. The translated dead weren't human anymore. The rushing water didn't stop them — it didn't even slow them down. They gripped the sides of the steamboat with powerful arms. Being dead had given them strength beyond normal strength.

As one, the dead vanished inside the cabins. The sound of cracking and splintering wood echoed across the water. Then they were back, wielding pistols and cutlasses.

The army was armed.

Ronny and Dad were aboard now, swinging iron pipes like baseball bats. Three translated souls fell quickly before them. But in moments, they crawled to their feet again. The dead were back up.

I couldn't watch anymore. I found myself neck-deep in the water, my arms flailing wildly toward the *Bellamina*. I felt her oily, slick, scummy, rotten planks and I pulled myself onto the deck.

"I hoped it wasn't true!" a voice said behind me. I turned, expecting the worst.

Bonton hobbled toward me, his eyes on fire. "I didn't want to believe it. Waldo is their captain. My precious boy! I have to try to stop him. . . ." He tore a piece of railing from a rotten stairway and stormed off, shouting at the top of his lungs. His false foot didn't stop him, just as age hadn't stopped Bob Lemon.

"Wait!" I cried. I spotted a cutlass on the floor and grabbed it. I wasn't sure if anything could stop the dead, but I had to try. Bonton and I moved together toward the main hall of the ship, where Ronny and Dad were.

A whistle sliced through the air. We turned. The bayou dogs stood panting on the deck behind us, heads low, teeth bared. Waldo stood behind them.

His small face twisted in anger. "You simple old man!" he crowed at Bonton, his voice even deeper than before. "Did you really think I was your son — all these years?"

Bonton was torn with rage and sorrow. "You —"

Before he could finish, Waldo whistled again and the dogs rippled across the air, skeletal beasts. Bonton screamed. I was there fast, chopping the air with the old sword. The dogs, untranslated, as immaterial as ghosts, leaped right through my blade.

"You little creep!" I shouted at Waldo.

Waldo laughed, then rushed at us. I held the old sword steady, but Waldo lunged low and arched up with his bony arms. My cutlass swung wildly to the side, struck the wall, snapped, and fell to the floor. Bonton grabbed the boy and pulled him off me.

Saber bloodied, saber broken, saber buried, burned, reborn . . .

Waldo scrambled to his feet as I jabbed out with the broken sword. At the same time, Bonton threw himself between us.

"No!" I cried.

Bonton screamed. He dropped his wooden stake and staggered from the room. My blade had struck him.

Insane with anger, I turned back to Waldo, but he darted away. "Don't worry, we'll meet again, mystery boy!" he snarled. The dogs bounded out of sight behind him.

Mystery boy? I had no time to wonder what he meant, because Ronny stumbled into the hall. In one hand was his length of iron piping. A swatch of ragged wet cloth dangled from it. In the other hand, he held an old flintlock pistol by its barrel.

"Above you —" he cried.

One of the smugglers, now in cargo shorts and sneakers, leaped down from the gallery above the main hall. My shoulder blade stung with sudden pain. I dropped to my knees.

The dead man arched for a second blow, but Ronny swung the pipe like a machine. The guy's arm flew across the room. There was a howl — not of pain, but of anger. Ronny fought the creature away from me. I wanted to cry out, but there was no time. We couldn't stop fighting.

Two more dead men appeared. One still had a camera dangling from his neck. They rushed at me. I slipped on the mucky deck and fell against the wall. It cracked into splinters, and I tumbled onto a set of stairs, losing the broken saber. The stairs burst their boards, and I dropped hard into a room on a lower deck.

"Ronny!" I shouted. But then a tourist — a teenager not quite as old as Ronny — was thrown down next to me by one of the gray-faced men.

"What's happening?" the boy asked me.

I knew what was happening. The dead needed drowning victims to translate into.

"We have to get off this boat!" I said.

The dead man lingered at the top of the stairs for a moment, saw me, turned, and walked away. Why?

I didn't have to wait long for the answer.

"What's hap —" the boy started again. A shape rose from the submerged far side of the room, dripping water from invisible shoulders.

"Get out of here!" I yelled to the boy. "Run. Run!" I tried to push him toward the broken stairs, but we both slipped and splashed into the water again. I knew what the shape wanted.

"Get out —"

I pulled the boy to his feet and shoved him toward a small door behind us. My foot dragged on the floor, caught the doorframe, and I tripped. The door slammed shut, trapping us both inside the room. Water was up to our waists.

The shape made no noise, moving unstoppably toward us.

The boy grabbed my arm, not understanding.

The thing lunged at us.

NINETEEN

The Meaning of Dreams

But not at me.

No.

The shape twisted in midair with the speed of lightning. It leaped at the terrified boy. I grabbed for him, missed. The soul and the boy disappeared underwater.

I knew what came next.

The water churned, bubbled, calmed. I knew it would. I had seen it before.

I knew what came next. Is that what Dad meant?

Had I seen a translation before?

I dug my feet into the floor, moved quickly along the wall, and made my way to the door on the far side of the room. Pausing for breath, I looked back. The boy rose out of the water. For an instant my heart broke. His eyes were dead, his skin without color. He sloshed toward me, a new foot soldier for the Legion.

I pushed through the door and scrambled up to the

main deck. Ronny and Dad were standing there together, exhausted, angry, horrified, but ready for more. The battle wasn't over.

Erskine Cane moved his hulking, gray-faced bulk onto the main deck. Behind him were the original dead from the Bordelon crash. His wife. The one-armed conductor. The gray-haired man. Twitchy. The others.

And forty new ones.

Their voices in my ear were deafening, but over it all I heard a scratchy laugh. The Legion parted. Waldo stood there, laughing like a mad, old soul.

"Derek Stone," he began. "Have you discovered —"

"Shut up!" I cried. I didn't want to hear his voice a second longer. Tearing the wooden angel out of my pocket, I ran at Waldo. My legs — chunky, worn out, bruised beyond belief — carried me past the dead. I was on him in seconds.

I smashed the angel into his face with all my strength. He shrieked. The angel shattered in my hands. Waldo fell to his knees, groaning, while something clanked and splashed to the deck at my feet.

It was a rusty iron key. I snatched it up.

Seeing it in my hand, Waldo exploded in anger.

And the dead swarmed.

TWENTY

On the Move

The dead didn't get far. With a roar, Bonton's airboat whumped over the capsized tour boats and thudded onto the *Bellamina*'s deck. It crashed through the sodden rails and into the main hall, propeller spinning wildly.

"Don't you dead ones come any closer!" Bonton shouted from the pilot's seat. With a swift turn of the wheel, he lurched the boat around so that the blades were flashing like a giant open fan between us and the dead. "Unless you want to be sliced to bits and fried up for supper!"

Still bleeding from his forehead, Bonton also clutched a giant flare gun.

Waldo let out a cry like a strangled wolf. His eyes bulged as he stared, frozen, at the rusted key in my hand. He wanted it.

The Legion waited.

My heart leaped into my throat. It was a standoff — the four of us against an army of the dead. We could do little against them, but they couldn't move any closer.

The propeller's blades whirred madly.

Cane grunted. The Legion turned. I guessed they had gotten what they came for — more bodies. They didn't get me. But there was always the next time. Now nearly fifty strong, they piled off the deck and onto the soaked ground, where the floodwater had leveled out.

As the airboat's propellers spun, we watched them disappear into the night. Before they vanished, Waldo whistled. The ghostly dogs raced through the trees, to his side.

The voices ebbed in my ear, but sirens crisscrossed one another, moving toward us. The *thuck-thuck* of helicopters battered the air overhead.

The police — and whoever else — had arrived.

Dad grabbed my shoulders. "You have to keep moving," he said. "No matter what happens, remember that I love you, even if you don't see me for a while —"

"Dad, no!" I said. "This is crazy. You're *not* going away again —"

He stared at the key in my hand. The handle was a scalloped oval with a flower shape inside. The teeth at the end of the barrel were oddly notched. It was old.

"What is this?" I asked him. "What does it open?"

Dad released his grip on me and pulled away slowly. "I don't know. But we can't let the police find us together," he said. "To stop the Legion we need to split up, here and now. I'll find you again, I promise. Right now, I'll distract the police. Get out of here —"

"Dad, please, no! You can't be a hit-and-run dad! You can't go. You have to —"

"You need to be free!" he shouted, turning to shore. "This war has been going on for a long time, and we're in the middle of it now. We might also be there at the end of it, if we do what we can. If *you* do what *you* can, Derek." He jumped into the water, waded to land, and stomped off in the rain. He began to run loudly through the trees, drawing the gleam of searchlights after him.

"*If* I *do what* I *can?*" I muttered. "All I can do is run."

That's when Bonton fell out of the pilot's seat.

"Bonton!" cried Ronny. We ran to him. The man's eyes were silvery. He moaned, lifting his hands to the great gash on the side of his head.

TWENTY-ONE

Staying Alive

We carried Bonton to the top of the levee and set him down. I thought of how we'd left Bob Lemon in the dark house. It seemed so long ago. There were fewer of us every minute.

I tried to prop his head up, but Bonton waved me away. "You helped me enough, Derek," he said. "You kept the dead away from me. I'll go natural. That's a blessing. It's okay for me now. I'll go soon."

"No —" I said.

Grimacing, he shook his head. "That night years ago, Derek, I heard the dogs, but came too late to save you. Someone already had. Stuffed in your pocket, dry as can be, was this." He dug his hand in the lining of his prosthetic boot and slid out a plastic bag with a folded yellow envelope inside. "Maybe you'll know what it means."

Bonton made a noise then. His face twisted in pain, then eased slowly, the lines and creases fading away.

He was gone.

Trembling, I opened the envelope. Inside was a wrinkled photograph. I knew from the train books in my father's collection that it was an early photograph, from around 1850 or so, before the Civil War. The image was small, but detailed and clear.

It was a plantation house. A huge old mansion with columns across the front, a deep porch, and a gallery across the second floor with a wrought-iron railing. Ivy covered one side of the house, and wisps of Spanish moss hung down over an iron fence in the foreground.

The scrollwork in the fence was flower-shaped, the same as on the handle of the iron key.

All of the details in the photograph were various shades of brown, but the house itself was hand-colored with a crimson wash. I remembered what Abby had told me on the phone earlier that day.

"The red house," I blurted out.

"What?" asked Ronny, glancing at the photograph.

"The red house," I repeated, looking at the key and wondering why it had been hidden in my house. "Abby told me the dead are heading there. They're looking for someone or something."

I heard more sirens and shouts pulling away from us on the other side of the swamp. Dad was leading the police on a chase. Maybe he'd escape. Maybe he'd get caught. I didn't know. I hadn't seen his hand, so I wasn't sure who or what he even was now, but he was helping us stay free.

Ronny pulled me to my feet. "The police will find Bonton and take care of him," he said, scanning the receding water. "Maybe they'll even piece together what happened here. They'll find another explanation for it. *Any* other explanation. But they're part of it now. It's getting bigger. We have to keep moving."

So. It was Ronny and me. Alone again.

But maybe there was someone else to think about, too.

I made one final call on my cell before the battery died completely. Before I got three words out, Abby cut me off.

"Meet me at the train station in Baton Rouge," she said. "Tomorrow at noon. I know where the red house is."

My heart skipped. "Tell me. I'm ready for anything."

"Not for this," she said, her voice faltering. "Meet me at the station. I have to tell you in person. There's something you don't —"

The phone went dead.

I turned to Ronny. "We're going to Baton Rouge."

He searched my face. "Why?" he asked. "To do what?"

I opened my mouth, but closed it again. I had no answer. Not that Ronny, for all his questions, seemed to expect one. He knew that no matter what we might imagine, the answers would be more terrifying than we could possibly believe. But we needed to know the truth, no matter how awful.

The water roared before us, and the giant black steamboat tilted, throwing waves up all around it. It had released its centuries-old dead. It was done. Slowly it leaned, sank into the black floodwater, and was gone at last.

Ronny looked straight up through the trees at the night sky. "More rain coming."

"You sound like Waldo," I said — then regretted it.

"I *am* like Waldo," he snapped, tapping his chest with his blackened finger. "And more rain *is* coming, so be ready. Night isn't over yet. We'd better move. I won't be here forever."

Making sure the old key was safely in my pocket, I followed Ronny to Waldo's rowboat. We climbed in and let it drift past the cemetery, the vault of trees, the shack, everything, until we reached Samantha's car. It was more mangled from Ronny's driving than I remembered. Maybe if Sam knew what was going on, she'd want us to keep the car as long as we needed it. When it wouldn't run anymore, she'd want us to find another and another, just to keep the horror away as long as possible.

Any sane person would.

Ronny started the car, and an hour later we were out of the bayous, heading north to Baton Rouge.

So this is life now. Home is gone. Family is gone. The army of the dead is growing, making their way across the land. Normal doesn't exist for me anymore.

Soon it won't exist for anyone else, either.

The old way of life is over.

This is war.

Don't miss the next volume in Derek's story . . .

The Red House

Read on for a special sneak peek!

The Red House

"He died."

Two words, and my dumb little life changed forever.

Six letters, and the world I believed in vanished into nothing, like fog.

"I won't believe it!" I cried, falling to my knees. "I won't!"

"You must believe it," was the stone cold reply.

As sunny and warm as the day began, night dropped hard and fast like the lid of a coffin.

The horror of it made me sick. I didn't want to go on. I *couldn't* go on.

I mean, how would *you* feel if someone told you —

Wait.

You couldn't possibly know how you'd feel unless you understood — really understood — what I'm talking about.

So let me wipe the blood from my forehead and go back nine hours to this morning.

I'll tell you everything that happened from that moment to now. You need to know where we came from, to understand where we are now.

We? Right. Let me start there.

My name is Derek Stone. I'm fourteen, fat, smarter than most people I know, and on the run. Nine hours ago, my older brother, Ronny, and I were holed up in a filthy room in a fleabag hotel on the outskirts of Baton Rouge, Louisiana. We'd been there since four a.m. the night before.

I opened my eyes. It was 11:21 a.m. The blinds were down, but sunlight sliced through them like a hot knife through butter. The air was a white haze. The room was an oven.

"How'd you pick this dump, anyway?" I asked Ronny, rolling off the mattress and onto my feet. "I feel horrible."

"You look horrible," Ronny snorted from the bathroom sink. "Being on the run means being on a budget. Our money's almost out."

I flipped open my cell. Black screen. Dead battery.

"I wish I could charge this thing," I said. "In case Abby calls again."

Abby Donner. My phone had died last night in the middle of a call from her.

More on her later.

"Dump that thing," said Ronny. "The cops can trace it, right? Besides, Abby's train comes in half an hour. Get dressed."

I pulled on my pants and shirt and muscled Ronny out of the bathroom. I held my breath as he passed.

Why did I hold my breath? Because Ronny is decaying.

"Decaying?" you say. "The dude's only nineteen. How could he be decaying? Only corpses do that, right?"

Right. Only corpses.

Man, I'm tired of telling this story. But you need to hear it. Your life depends on it, though you may not know it yet. So listen up, and bear with me. There's a lot to tell, and not much time.

A few weeks ago Ronny, my father, and I were in a bad train wreck. Maybe you heard about it. Big news. The old bridge over Bordelon Gap collapsed. Our train fell into the ravine. Ronny was one of nine passengers killed.

Then he came back.

Came back?

Trust me, that's the easy part.

"We're out of here," Ronny said. He pulled me into the hotel hallway with all my worldly possessions: twenty-something dollars, twenty pounds of extra fat, a headache, and a case of the shakes.

"Let's skidaddle," he added.

Skidaddle? That's exactly what I'm talking about.

Ronny came back from the train wreck — at least, his body did. Inside him was the soul of a young man named Virgil Black. Virgil died in an almost identical train crash at the same place back in 1938. Because the two accidents were so alike, and because the curtain that separates the worlds of the living and the dead has been torn — I call it the *Rift* — souls in the afterlife were able to enter the crash victims at the moment they died.

"*Enter* the crash victims?" you say.

Yep. Reanimate them.

Like, "Hello! We're back!"

It's the old body, but a different soul. I call this grotesque soul-switching *translation*.

Another one of the train wreck victims was my father. He was missing for weeks, presumed dead, since all they could find of him was his finger. But then he turned up alive and *un*translated . . . I think.

The souls who came back are a pack of notorious convicts, led by a murderous thug called Erskine Cane. I'd learned pretty quickly that these dark souls are only the advance troops of a huge, massive dead-guy army called the Legion.

The Legion.

The word makes me nauseous.

"Come on," Ronny said, slinging his small bag into the trunk of a beat-up green Subaru that belonged to his ex-girlfriend, Samantha. It had looked much nicer before we'd borrowed it. "Clock's ticking." I slid into the passenger seat.

According to Ronny — er, Virgil — for centuries, the evil souls of the Legion have been warring against good souls in the afterlife. And they're winning. Once they discovered the Rift, they began translating into dead bodies and bringing their war up here.

Why?

To take over.

"I don't like this," Ronny said. He slowed the car and pulled over to the curb to let four police cruisers tear past us.

"You don't think they know about us, do you?" I said.

"Maybe," he said quietly. "Maybe Uncle Carl told them to look for us." The police cars roared up the street and away. After a minute, Ronny pulled back into traffic.

My father's brother Carl had stayed with me in New Orleans after the train crash. He was there when Ronny came back, but he didn't know the whole story. He just thought Ronny was out of sorts, traumatized. He couldn't have imagined the truth. Uncle Carl was out of town when Erskine Cane burned down our house in the French Quarter.

Ronny and I had been hiding out ever since. It was only a matter of time before the cops got involved, really. With a mass translation in the bayou, with Dad leading the cops on a wild goose chase so we could get away, with people "dying" and then mysteriously "coming back," the cops would soon be all over our war with the dead.

The war, I called it.

Simple, but effective.

"I'll park a few blocks from the station, just to be safe," Ronny said. Then he snorted. "Safe? Some joke, huh?"

Neither one of us was laughing.

"Here we are." Ronny stopped the Subaru at a curb three and a half blocks from the train station. "Hurry it up, Tubs."

There's love for you. One of the weirdest things about Ronny is that even though he's Virgil Black now — a farm boy from upstate in Shongaloo — there are still bits of Ronny in him. An occasional look. A phrase. A gesture. Something.

So I still call him Ronny.

Virgil doesn't seem to mind.

I followed him along the sidewalk. It was 11:51 a.m. Our day had begun.

Abby's train was due at noon, and it was four minutes to twelve by the time we arrived in the main concourse of the train station.

Almost the first thing I saw was the blazer.

Navy blue, shiny, saggy in the shoulders, with a bulge under the left arm. And then another blazer just like it, and another, and another. Between and above the baggy shoulders were thick necks, sweaty foreheads, and darting eyes.

"Police?" I said. "Federal agents?"

Ronny glanced furiously from face to face as the men moved quickly into every corner of the large room. "This is bad. If they bring us in, they won't believe a word we say, and the Legion will keep growing until it's too late. Slip into the shadows. If I lose you, I'll meet you on the street behind the building. Keep out of sight. We may have to start running."

Running? That loosened something in my head, and strange words echoed from my memory.

Children of light, lost, so lost, running in darkness . . .

I shivered to hear those words in my mind. Like other words I'd "heard" since the accident, I had no clue what these meant. But they sure seemed to be about Ronny and me.

. . . lost, so lost, running in darkness . . .

And maybe Abby, too.

Ronny pulled me out of the main room, toward platform 13. We ducked into a bagel shop when a couple of guys in blazers passed.

"Uh-oh, Ronny," I whispered. "Look up there."

A flat-screen TV behind the counter showed grainy nighttime footage of water rushing through a bayou.

Malpierre. I knew it.

My chest buzzed when a TV voiceover began describing the incident. I couldn't hear everything, but I could hear enough. "Flash flood . . . broken lock . . . crested levees . . . bayou tour boats . . . startling rescue . . ." The video then showed a car hidden among the bayou overgrowth.

Our green Subaru.

"That's it," Ronny said. "They must have spotted the car outside. They're closing in. There's her train."

The train from New Orleans squealed to a stop, and right away, the platform was flooded with passengers. We waited in the bagel shop, scanning the crowd. Almost the last person to leave the train was a girl with long brown hair tied in a loose ponytail. Abby Donner. She wore blue shorts and a green T-shirt, and had a big handbag slung over her shoulder.

Abby had broken her ankle in the train wreck a month ago, but when she walked down the platform, I saw that her ankle cast was gone. She was using a wooden cane.

"I'm going," I said.

"Wait for her to come a little closer —" Ronny grabbed my arm.

"I'm going." I pushed out of the shop and walked quickly to the platform, head down, hoping no one would notice me.

TONY ABBOTT is the author of more than seventy books for young readers, including the bestselling The Secrets of Droon series and the novels *Kringle*, *Firegirl* (winner of the 2006 Golden Kite Fiction Award), and most recently *The Postcard*. The Haunting of Derek Stone is his third series for Scholastic. It combines Tony's fascination with the Southern Gothic tradition, a long-held pessimism about the future of our delicate world, and a basic love of spooky stories. He lives and writes in Connecticut with his wife, two daughters, and their corgi, Comet. Visit him online at **www.tonyabbottbooks.com**.